PRAISE FOR THE REVEREND ANNABELLE DIXON COZY MYSTERY SERIES

"Absolutely wonderful!!"
"I read it that night, and it was GREAT!"
"I couldn't put it down!"
"4 thumbs up!!!"
"It kept me up until 3am. I love it."
"As a former village vicar this ticks the box for me."
"This series keeps getting better and better."
"Annabelle, with her great intuition, caring personality, yet imperfect judgment, is a wonderful main character."
"It's fun to grab a cup of tea and pretend I'm sitting in the vicarage discussing the latest mysteries with Annabelle while she polishes off the last of the cupcakes."
"Great book - love Reverend Annabelle Dixon and can't wait to read more of her books."
"Annabelle reminds me of Agatha Christie's Miss Marple."
"A perfect weekend read."
"I LOVE ANNABELLE!"
"A wonderful read, delightful characters and if that's not enough the sinfully delicious recipes will have you coming back for more."

"This cozy series is a riot!"

BODY IN THE WOODS

ALSO BY ALISON GOLDEN

Death at the Café

Murder at the Mansion

Body in the Woods

Grave in the Garage

Horror in the Highlands

Killer at the Cult

Fireworks in France

COLLECTIONS

Books 1-4

Death at the Café

Murder at the Mansion

Body in the Woods

Grave in the Garage

Books 5-7

Horror in the Highlands

Killer at the Cult

Fireworks in France

BODY IN THE WOODS

ALISON GOLDEN

JAMIE VOUGEOT

Cover Illustration: Rosalie Yachi Clarita

Published by Mesa Verde Publishing
P.O. Box 1002
San Carlos, CA 94070

Edited by
Marjorie Kramer

"It is never too late to be what you might have been."
George Eliot

To get the first books in each of my series - *Chaos in Cambridge, The Case of the Screaming Beauty, Hunted, and Mardi Gras Madness* - plus updates about new releases, promotions, and other Insider exclusives, please sign up for Alison's mailing list at:

https://www.alisongolden.com/annabelle

CHAPTER ONE

I T HAD BEEN a tough week for young Master Douglas "Dougie" Dewar. It had begun with him tearing his school uniform during a particularly ambitious tree-climbing adventure, continued with reprisals about his over-active imagination from his teacher Miss Montgomery, and reached its peak when Aunt Shona discovered he had been trying to rustle sheep by training none other than the church cat, a ginger tabby named Biscuit.

How could they blame him? He had been in Upton St. Mary for only four months since his mother had sent him there from their home in Edinburgh, and he still found the village and the vibrant countryside surrounding it full of possibilities.

He would trek the rolling hills armed only with a trusty stick and an insisted-upon sandwich, imagining himself a brave adventurer on a quest to find a wise, old wizard. He would swing from tree branches like a wilderness warrior, announcing his presence with a signature yell, determined to save all of civilization, reaping world domination as his prize. And he would creep through the dense forest, envisioning it as some deep, exotic jungle on a strange new planet, while encountering delicate, well-camouflaged wildlife that demonstrated all the curiosity and nervousness of timid alien visitors.

For Dougie was not just energetic and rambunctious of body, but of mind as well. When he wasn't scampering through the rolling countryside in search of adventures, he was poring over pages of the most astonishing and outlandish tales he could find, stoking the fires of his imagination before he lived out his fantasies against Cornwall's glorious pastoral background.

Oh yes, it had been a tough week indeed, but it had also been an incredibly fun one.

Now it was Friday, and the glorious feeling of being on the precipice of the weekend's adventures had Dougie running wildly through the forest on his way home from school. After his mishap earlier in the week, Aunt Shona had insisted he change out of his uniform when he got home before embarking on his adventures. It was a small price to pay, thought Dougie, as he darted, jumped, and swerved around the various tree trunks. But he wasn't home yet.

"No more school," he shouted, as he deftly switched his weight from one foot to another to avoid slipping on a tree root. "No more Miss Montgomery!" As he kept on running, he ran through his weekend plans. "I'll meet the boys to play football tomorrow, and then Aunt Shona promised me a trip to the bookstore. Gonna get the next in the 'Reptiloid Hunter' series. Woo-hoo!"

His imagination ran wild with excitement. He ducked his head and pictured himself a spaceship shooting through an asteroid field. He skipped off a bank and fancied himself on a flying carpet. He spread his arms and turned sharply like a fighter jet, his school satchel sailing behind him like a tail.

Just as he was about to bank sharply again and release another barrage of missiles, however, Dougie found himself genuinely floating in mid-air, his feet up behind him. For a split second, he almost believed he was flying.

"Oof!" he grunted as he landed on his chest atop the tough late summer soil.

Dougie bounced back up almost immediately, his youthful exuberance overwhelming the sharp pain in his elbow and the winded sensation in his chest.

"Oh no! I'm going to be grounded for a week!" he cried as he looked down at the dirt and grass firmly embedded into his school uniform. Cautiously, he checked the spot where the stinging sensation was coming from on his elbow.

"Noooooo!" was all Dougie could muster. He had been well-schooled in the art of politeness and not even being alone in the middle of the woods was enough for him to forget his good manners and utter anything ruder – however much the frayed tear on his blazer warranted it.

He spun around, his pained expression turning to one of anger. Whichever tree root was responsible was going to get it. He took a few steps toward the spot at which he tripped and scanned for the offending object.

The thin, bar-like protrusion which jutted out of the ground at a low angle was not like any tree root Dougie had ever seen. In fact, he had never come across anything remotely like it on his treasure hunts across the forest. He knelt and brushed some of the dirt away.

As he uncovered more of the thin, white oddity, Dougie's heart seemed to sink lower, until it turned a somersault. He knew what this was. They had studied the human skeleton just last week in class.

Dougie's mouth opened slowly as he stared at the bone, his mind searching for another, less terrifying prospect. Suddenly, he found himself out of all other potential explanations and incredibly afraid. He hopped to his feet and sprinted toward Aunt Shona's cottage – only this time he was trying to stifle his imagination rather than explore it.

"The boy's fine," Shona Alexander assured her sister on the phone, "he's a little scamp. With a boy like him you only need to worry when he's *not* up to something... Oh, of course he misses you. He asks after you every chance he gets... He's still so distracted by the excitement of a new place... You've got enough to worry about right now with the chemo, Olivia, just let me take care of Dougie for now... Oh, wait, I think I hear him coming in. I'll get him to call you later, okay? Bye, Olivia."

Shona placed the receiver down gently and turned around.

"That was your mot—"

"Aunt Shona!"

Shona and Dougie stared at each other, each bearing an expression of absolute horror.

"Good Lord, Dougie! Look at you!"

"There's a.... There's... It's... I don't know why it's there!"

"Is that a rip? Turn around! Turn around, now! Oh dear Lord..."

"No, Aunt Shona... I saw a... It was right there!"

"What was?"

"A... It looked like... There's a... There's a dead body in the woods!"

"Oh, there'll be a dead body in the woods, alright, if you don't explain to me how you made a mess of yourself when I specifically told you not to go running about before coming home to change."

"Really, Aunt Shona! There's a bone sticking out!"

"Sticking out of where?"

"Out of the ground! I tripped over it!"

Shona placed two hands upon her hips and circled Dougie as if inspecting a car she was considering buying. She shook her head as she noticed every stain, assessing how much time it would take to get each one out.

"You really do have quite an imagination. I hope you realize this means you won't be playing soccer this weekend, young man!"

Dougie stamped his foot impertinently and cried out desperately. "I don't care about the football! There's a dead body in the woods!"

Bizarrely, Shona found Dougie's first statement more surprising than the second, and when she saw the earnestness in the boy's face, she realized that he meant both of them sincerely. Dougie certainly attracted more than his fair share of trouble, but if anything, it was his open, impulsive nature that drew him to it, rather than his proclivity to spin tall tales.

"Sit down," Shona commanded the boy, as she pulled out a chair and sat on it. "Tell me exactly what happened."

Inspector Mike Nicholls was in no mood for games and hadn't been for a while. He had grumbled and complained his way through each workday for over two weeks, and yet his fellow officers had grown none the wiser as to the cause.

Nothing out of the ordinary had happened, and the incidents they had dealt with were remarkable only in their consistency and mildness. Even the weather hadn't been so bad. Yet not even a cup of tea could be served to the Detective Inspector without vociferous criticism about its sweetness or lack thereof. He did not hold back expounding on any other grievance he found pertaining to the cup in question, either. The tea might be too hot, too cold, too strong, or the wrong kind of brew entirely. Officers within his vicinity were liable to receive spiked comments about their manner or work ethic, and even those not present would be noted for their absence, the reasons for which were undoubtedly nefarious in the Inspector's newly negative outlook.

So when the call came from Constable Raven that drove the Inspector to leave the city for the countryside immediately, the officers of Truro police station breathed a sigh of relief before drawing straws to decide who would go with him. Constable Colback drew the short one.

After a long trip, during which Inspector Nicholls articulated his grievances on topics as wide-ranging as long car journeys, people wasting police time, the declining standards of police ceremonies, and the road manners of his fellow drivers, he and his bedraggled constable met the local village bobby, Constable Raven, outside Shona Alexander's house.

"Hello Inspector! Long time no see," said Constable Raven, more cheerily than the grave circumstances demanded.

"I have a forensic team on standby, Constable," the Inspector responded curtly. "So I sincerely hope this is not a waste of time."

Picking up on the Inspector's unusually stern tone, Raven stood upright.

"I don't think so, Inspector. Ms. Alexander and Dougie, her young nephew, sound very concerned."

"How old's the boy?" the Inspector asked.

"I believe he's eight, sir," Raven replied.

"Wait a minute, Constable," Nicholls said, a dark cloud passing over his face. "Are you telling me that I've just put all my other duties aside, made a formal request for the forensic team to enter the area, and driven for almost an hour, based on the story that a schoolboy told his aunt? You didn't check the site yourself?"

Constable Raven struggled to disguise his gulp. He was an informal but effective officer, though diligence and rigor had never been his strengths. Under the intense glare of the Inspector, he suddenly wished they were.

"I didn't want to disturb the scene, Inspector. I thought it right that you be here to witness it first."

DI Nicholls winced, opened his mouth to say something, decided against it, and walked up the pathway to Shona Alexander's door, leaving Constables Raven and Colback to exchange sympathetic glances.

"I'm Detective Inspector Nicholls," he said to the blonde woman who opened the door, "I believe you are Ms. Shona Alexander and this lad is Dougie Dewar?"

"Yes, thank you for coming, Inspector."

The Inspector crouched, bringing himself to eye-level with the freshly-washed boy who clung to his aunt's trouser leg.

"What did you see out there, boy?"

After a few seconds, Dougie gathered up the courage to speak.

"There was this bone. An arm bone, sticking out of the ground. I tripped on it and got mud and dirt all over me."

"How big?"

Dougie raised his hands and held them about four inches apart. Nicholls looked around to cast another stern glare at Constable Raven.

"Now are you sure it wasn't a twig? A strange stick, or maybe something plastic?"

Dougie shook his head, too intimidated by the Inspector's direct, unyielding approach to speak.

"A lot of animals have bones, you know. Tell me why you think this was a human bone? An arm, you say?"

"I studied the skeleton at school last week. It has a curve like this," Dougie said, proudly tracing his finger along his forearm, "and another bone next to it like this. That's what it looked like."

Nicholls sighed deeply.

"Well, let's get to it then. The young lad can show us the path and tell us about it on the way."

The detective stood up and began walking back down the path, followed by Dougie and his Aunt Shona. As he passed Constable Raven, he glowered once again and said:

"I hope this kid's knowledge of anatomy is better than your knowledge of police procedure, Constable. For all our sakes."

The sky was turning a dark shade of orange as the five figures approached the long shadows of the woods. Though the days still bore the pleasant warmth and brightness of summer, the sharp decrease in temperature as the sun set over the hills indicated that the warm season was about to be chased away. There was a little crunch in the rustle of leaves underfoot, and the fervent greens that rolled away in all directions began to wane into shades less vivid as encroaching hues of brown and yellow made themselves apparent.

Though Dougie was meant to lead them, he shuffled along beside his Aunt Shona, clutching her hand, while Inspector Nicholls strode forward, setting a brisk pace. Constables Raven and Colback brought up the rear, chatting a little and scanning the surroundings purposefully when they thought Nicholls was watching.

DI Nicholls turned to Dougie as they passed through another clump of trees and began to navigate the deepening shade of the dense forest. Dougie, still rather intimidated by the Inspector's intense silence, raised his arm and pointed ahead, a little to one side. Nicholls nodded once and continued onwards determinedly.

"There!" Dougie squealed suddenly. "That's where I fell! So the bone is..."

Everyone watched the boy's finger trace a trajectory in the air until it pointed to a spot on the ground. Dougie stepped back and pressed himself up against Aunt Shona's trouser leg once again.

DI Nicholls almost leaped toward the spot Dougie had indicated, followed closely by the two constables. They gazed at the strange protrusion for a few seconds, musing over its unusual shape.

"Take the woman and the boy to the edge of the forest, Colback. It's a little way over. You can meet the forensic team there if we need them. Constable Raven?"

"Yes sir?"

"Help me dig it out a little – carefully."

"Yes sir."

As Shona walked after Constable Colback, pulling Dougie away and holding his head so that he couldn't look back, Nicholls and Raven pulled away at the dirt from which the bone emerged. After almost ten minutes of clawing at the ground, growing increasingly impatient, they unearthed what was unmistakably a human elbow.

DI Nicholls pulled out his phone.

"Colback? Call in the forensic team, and bring them over. Tell them we've confirmed it."

Within the hour, night had fallen swiftly and Upton St. Mary had become shrouded in darkness. Drivers on the lazily curving country lanes had to depend on their headlights to see, and the quaint cottages and houses were apparent only by the warm glow coming from their windows and visitor lamps. Few people were outside, most choosing to enjoy the comfort and warmth of their homes, but for those who were, the sky was clear enough for moonlight to help them along their way.

Tonight, however, there were vibrant additions supplementing Upton St. Mary's nighttime illuminations. Multiple police cars had parked by the wall of trees at the woods' edge, their blue lights casting ominous blinking shadows across the forest floor. A little deeper in the woods, powerful lamps, set up by the forensic team, cast a piercing white glare over the scenes of crime officers as they carefully excavated and examined the forest floor. Police officers circled the area, scanning for clues or merely making their way through the unlit portions of the woods, directing their flashlight beams erratically like they were roving spotlights.

There would be gossip in the morning for sure, thought DI Nicholls, as he marched back toward the woods from Shona Alexander's house. He had really needed that cup of tea, but his lengthy conversation with Dougie and Shona had not revealed much. The boy had been more concerned with the mess he had made of his uniform, while his aunt seemed to live an incredibly isolated life at the big stone cottage, sentimentally named "Honeysuckle House." Despite living for fifteen years in Upton St. Mary, the closest she had come to giving him a lead was information concerning a land dispute that had been resolved eighteen months ago.

"Damnit!" Nicholls exclaimed into the dark night as he stubbed his boot on a large rock, almost stumbling head over heels. "Bloody rock!"

"You should have a torch," came a distant voice.

Nicholls looked up and was blinded by a powerful beam.

"Get that light out of my eyes!" he cried, angrily.

The beam was lowered, and as his eyes adjusted once again to the darkness, Nicholls saw the svelte figure of Harper Jones emerging from a cluster of trees.

"Sorry," DI Nicholls growled, as she drew closer, "I didn't realize it was you, Harper."

Not many people could elicit an apology from the Inspector, but Harper Jones demanded a certain respect, not least because she was one of the most brilliant pathologists in Britain and thus the Inspector's best hope for making some sense of the dead body in the woods.

Harper reached the Inspector and dropped her flashlight to her side. Even in the dim light, the Inspector could make out Harper's attractive face and upright bearing from the slivers of fading light that outlined her sharp features.

"This body's been here a while," Harper announced rather obviously, never one for small talk.

"How long?" the Inspector asked.

"We'll definitely need some time to figure it out. We're

still excavating it as carefully as possible, but my guess is that it's been buried there for well over a decade," she said.

"A decade?!"

Harper nodded, the moonlight skipping along her wavy hair. "Judging by the tissue quantities and the large number of roots that have grown around it. It's why the excavation still has some way to go."

Nicholls scratched his stubble and looked off toward the rhythmic blue glow being cast over the road.

"Is there anything else you can tell me?"

"Not much," Harper replied. "The body is in a fetal position, but that could mean anything. Defending against an attacker, huddling for warmth, disposal into a small hole – I don't know. That's your job."

Nicholls sighed deeply.

"We're never going to close a case this cold."

"There is one request I'd like to make," Harper said, maintaining her cool, assertive tone of voice despite her slight alarm at the Inspector's level of pessimism so early in the case.

"What's that?"

"I'd like a second opinion on this body. There's a lot of damage. It's difficult to ascertain what may be suspicious and what is the effect of decay, root growth, or simply the person's health in life. If I'm to make any judgments, I'd like the opinion of a forensic anthropologist."

"Do you have anybody in mind?"

For the first time, DI Nicholls detected a slightly regretful expression on the face of Harper Jones. He immediately dismissed it as a trick of the light, but Harper's somewhat wistful tone caused him to reconsider.

"Yes, actually."

"Okay. Well, bring them on board. I'm willing to pull in anyone who can help."

"That's good," Harper said, turning her head toward the road, "because I believe you're about to gain another ally."

Nicholls turned his head just in time to see a royal blue Mini Cooper pull up neatly behind a police car.

They watched as the large, unmistakable frame of Reverend Annabelle Dixon stepped out of the car and strode over to a nearby officer. After exchanging a few words, the constable gazed across the open stretch of land and pointed them out.

"Oh great," muttered Nicholls as Annabelle waved cheerily and began striding toward them, her smile visible even in the darkness. Harper raised her torch to reveal where they were, causing Annabelle to squint and stumble backward in its blinding glare.

"Don't be proud," Harper said quietly, as she turned back toward the woods. "The Reverend is a smart cookie – and you're going to need all the help you can get with this one."

DI Nicholls gazed at the looming figure of Annabelle coming toward him, arms in full marching mode. When she got close, she took one step too many and clattered into him.

"Oops!" she said, unconvincingly. "Terribly dark, isn't it?"

"I'm afraid I'm busy, Reverend."

"Whatever's going on, Inspector?"

"I can't tell you. It's police business and classified. The one thing I can tell you is that you'll have to move along."

Disregarding the Inspector's dismissive tone, Annabelle decided to keep probing.

"It looks serious," she remarked, turning her head

toward the bright lamps of the forensic team. "I hope nobody was hurt."

Nicholls remained silent.

Annabelle was rather fond of the Inspector, more than a little fond if the rumors were to be believed, but she found his silence somewhat rude and unfriendly. Not least because she had only recently helped the Inspector solve a particularly tricky case. Nonetheless, Annabelle, her big, warm heart nearly always bursting with generosity, was determined, happy even, to place the blame for the Inspector's grumpiness on his long drive from Truro.

"Do you know whose body it is?" asked Annabelle, matter-of-factly.

The lines of DI Nicholls' frown were so deep that they were visible even by the faint light of the moon.

"Who told you there's a body?!"

"Nobody!" Annabelle responded jovially. "I simply noticed the forensic team working busily away. There are only two things I can think of that would demand so many people be plugging away at the ground – the discovery of treasure or a dead body. And you don't need so many policemen to unearth treasure!"

Annabelle laughed easily, unable to notice the Inspector's scowl in the darkness.

"I'll hope you're not planning to go around telling people there's a dead body in the woods, Reverend."

"Heavens, no! But I don't imagine it'll be a secret for long."

"Why's that?"

"Well, this road gets rather busy in the morning. It's one of the main commuter routes. You'll have plenty of rubber-neckers spreading gossip before most people have had their morning coffee!"

Nicholls sighed defeatedly. He hated gossip, especially when it involved a case of his and even more so when it involved a case as open as this. Once it started, he would be stumbling upon more red herrings than one would find in a mystery novel.

"Goodbye, Reverend," DI Nicholls said, decisively.

"Bye, Inspector!"

Both of them took a step in opposite directions before DI Nicholls looked back.

"Reverend? Your car is that way."

"Oh I know, Inspector. I'm still on my daily rounds and thought I'd pay the good Ms. Alexander a visit."

Nicholls considered trying to dissuade the Reverend, but he knew her well enough to know it was a lost cause. He nodded grimly and headed back toward the forensic team.

Annabelle was not immune to the Inspector's bizarrely downbeat manner, and she could only surmise that whatever – or whoever – was buried in the woods behind Honeysuckle House was a cause for great concern. If anyone knew what was happening, it would be Shona Alexander, her bouncy young nephew being the only one who frequented those woods daily.

She walked briskly closer to the welcoming light of Honeysuckle House's decorated windows. Pots of herbs and aromatic flowers were neatly arranged beneath them. As she opened the wooden gate to Shona's wildflower garden, she noticed Constable Raven coming in the opposite direction.

"Constable Raven!"

"Oh, hello Reverend. Strange to see you out this late."

"It's not that late, Constable. The days are simply getting shorter."

Jim Raven looked up at the sky.

"I suppose you're right. It's going to get cold soon, I'd better get my boiler fixed."

"Constable," Annabelle said, seriously. "What is all this fuss about in the woods?"

Constable Raven shook his head slowly. "I'm sorry, Reverend. I'm under strict orders from Detective Inspector Nicholls to keep this as secret as possible."

"I had a feeling you might say that. But it must be something rather concerning to have the Inspector so worked up."

Raven allowed himself a wry smile. "Are you referring by chance to the chief's foul mood? I'm afraid that's got nothing to do with the case. He's been acting like he swallowed a wasp for weeks now."

"Why?" asked Annabelle, leaning forward with keen interest.

Raven shook his head.

"Constable Colback tells me nobody in Truro has the faintest idea what's bothering him. It's an even bigger mystery than the body in the woods. Ah—"

Raven stuttered, looking for something to say that would distract Annabelle from his slip of the tongue. Annabelle chuckled.

"Relax, Constable. I had already figured that out."

Raven's shoulders dropped a full inch, deflated. "It's nice of you to fib, Reverend, but I shouldn't have said that."

"Forget about it, Constable," Annabelle said, stepping past him. "I'll see you about the village, I expect."

"Yeah," muttered Constable Raven, still shaking his

head at his own stupidity. "You're not planning to ask Ms. Alexander about this, are you?"

Annabelle smiled. "I was actually planning to ask her how she was managing to keep her basil so vital at this time of year, but I expect this will be a rather unavoidable subject."

Constable Raven nodded as if receiving bad news, before turning around and making his way out of the garden and back toward the crime scene. As he went on his way, he decided that his spilling the beans was no fault of his own. It was Reverend Annabelle. She simply had a very sharp knack for uncovering secrets.

CHAPTER TWO

ANNABELLE RUNG THE doorbell and almost immediately heard Shona Alexander's Scottish brogue grow louder as she made her way to the door.

"I think this is quite enough for one night. I've already fallen behind on my chores. I've got an unbelievably muddy school uniform to mend, and — Oh! It's you, Reverend!" Shona's flustered face appeared at the door. Her expression had quickly turned to one of relief when she saw who was standing there. "I'm sorry, Reverend, I've just been run ragged by all these policemen and their questions. There are only so many times you can tell people that you don't know anything before you start going mad."

"I understand, Shona. Are you alright?"

"I'm fine, Reverend," Shona sighed. "I just need a little peace and quiet."

"Is Dougie holding up?"

"Oh, that little rascal," she said, gesturing the Reverend inside and closing the door, "he's indestructible. He was shaken more by the Inspector than the body, I think."

Annabelle nodded ruefully as she entered the kitchen and took a seat at the table. Shona picked up the kettle.

"Tea?"

"That would be lovely," cooed Annabelle.

"How are things at the church?" asked Shona as she sat down.

"They're ticking over smoothly," Annabelle said, "which is all you can really ask for. I think Philippa has been rather bored lately, honestly. The church accounts don't make for riveting reading at this time of year, not during the quiet time between the summer fête and the harvest festival. I'm sure she'll have plenty to talk about tomorrow though, once the news spreads. What about you?"

"Och," Shona said, waving the comment aside. "I've got more than enough to occupy my mind these days."

Annabelle noted the sadness in Shona's liquid-blue eyes. She was an attractive woman, though she had never married. After spending her formative years in Scotland, she had moved down to the south of England in order to pursue her passion for painting and pottery. Her family had been wealthy, and supportive, yet the young Shona Alexander was keen to strike out on her own. She had moved to Honeysuckle House, a property her family had owned for generations, full of excitement at her impending independence. But after years of only moderate success in her artistic endeavors, she had settled into a life of quiet routine; the odd exhibition in Truro, taking on the occasional commission, and more recently, the task of caring for her nephew.

Shona had always lived a life of her own design, but in recent years she had felt a lack of something profound, something larger than herself that she could dedicate herself toward. Her sister's illness had only added to her moroseness, and though the arrival of Dougie had offered plenty to occupy both her mind and hands, it had also reminded Shona of what she had been missing: companionship. She was lonely.

"How is your sister doing?" Annabelle asked softly.

"She'll be having a test next week to see, so I've got my fingers crossed."

"I'll say a prayer for her."

"Thank you, Reverend. I think she's finding the chemo tough."

Annabelle nodded solemnly. Shona stood up and got to work making the tea. Annabelle gazed at the paintings around the room. They were mainly watercolors that depicted the various familiar hills and locations of Upton St. Mary. She had always loved Shona's work, and indeed, had first become friends with her when commissioning a small piece that now hung in her church office.

"Annabelle!" squealed Dougie from the doorway.

"Hello, you!" Annabelle replied as the boy walked toward her.

"Dougie! Where are your manners? You're to call the Reverend, 'Reverend'."

"It's fine," Annabelle said, tousling the young boy's hair affectionately. "You've certainly been the center of attention today, haven't you Dougie?"

Dougie beamed proudly.

"I found a skeleton!"

"Dougie!" exclaimed Shona. "It was just a bone!"

"But I heard them *say* it was a skeleton!" Dougie asked, utterly confident in his assertion.

"Those insensitive police," muttered Shona disapprovingly. "They've only got their minds on their work and never think of how it affects people."

Annabelle smiled sympathetically.

"It's nothing to be afraid of," she said, half to Shona and half to Dougie. "Whoever is buried there died a very long time ago."

Shona brought the tea and biscuits to the table.

"What makes you say that, Reverend?"

"Well, they've been digging like a bunch of hyperactive moles all evening," Annabelle said, craning her neck to look out the window at the bright glow emanating from the woods, "and it looks like they're still at it. Whatever is in the ground, it's firmly planted there."

"The murderer could have dug a hole and put him in there last week! I saw it in a movie!"

"Dougie!"

Annabelle chuckled.

"Possibly, but then you would have tripped over a fleshy arm – not a bone, Dougie."

Dougie made a disgusted face and shook his head in an exaggerated motion. "Eurgh!"

"I've lived here for fifteen years," Shona said, thoughtfully, "and I've never heard of anybody going missing in the woods."

Annabelle shrugged.

"Maybe they've been there even longer than that. Or maybe it was a poor homeless person who froze to death."

"Makes me shiver to think what could be lying in the ground. Just on your doorstep."

"Maybe it's the ghost!" Dougie shouted, his eyes wide with excitement.

"Hush now, Dougie," Shona scolded, "whatever it is, it's none of our business now."

"Wait a minute," Annabelle said, a curious expression on her face, "did you say *the* ghost, Dougie?"

Dougie nodded, afraid to speak in case it resulted in more admonishments.

"You mean, there's rumors of a ghost in those woods?"

Dougie nodded again, his lips visibly pressed together, as if they would be compelled to speak if he didn't suppress them. He looked at Aunt Shona, who shrugged her permission for him to talk to Annabelle.

"Miss Montgomery's sister! She went missing in the woods a long, long time ago. Everyone thinks she died. Jack said he saw her running through there one time wearing a white dress. She looked much younger than Miss Montgomery, because she was only young when she disappeared. Ryan said it's because she went to see a film with a boy, but Angelina says that's rubbish because girls go to see films with boys all the time. She even dared Ryan to go to see a film with her to see if—"

"Miss Montgomery, your teacher?" Shona asked, knowing that unless she interrupted, Dougie would spin a story without an ending, forever and ever, amen.

Dougie nodded, gulping down air to catch his breath, so fast was his speech. "The one who told me off for doing my homework about Professor Xenomorph instead of the book she gave us. I didn't even read the book. Frank's teacher said that so long as you read, it doesn't matter what it is. Reading is itself a—"

"Okay, Dougie," Shona said, placing a hand over his arm and drawing him close to calm him down, "don't go getting all excited again. You'll never get to sleep. Why don't you go brush your teeth? I'll be up to read you a story as soon as I finish my tea."

"Bye Reverend!" Dougie shouted quickly, as if in an

incredible rush, his energy eager to be channeled into something, but his mind racing too quickly to find whatever that something might be.

Shona chuckled softly at the sound of his feet thumping quickly up the stairs.

"That boy has a mind that goes places as quickly and as randomly as his feet."

"Perhaps," uttered Annabelle slowly, lost in her own thoughts, "but I doubt he was lying about those rumors."

"Reverend, surely you don't think there's any value to them. They're just idle ghost stories! The kind of thing that children make up all the time about their teachers."

Annabelle nodded her agreement, but her eyes were still fixed somewhere in the distance of her thoughts.

"I suppose. Though even a broken clock is right twice a day."

Annabelle and Shona sipped the last of their tea simultaneously, before the Reverend slapped her knees and stood up.

"Well, I should get going. I'll drop by soon to see how you're getting on – though I'm sure you won't be bothered any more by all of this. It's purely a police matter now."

"You're welcome here anytime Annabelle. It was nice to see someone who wasn't wearing a uniform today."

Annabelle chuckled as she made her way to the door. Before she opened it, she turned and clasped Shona's hands in hers.

"Send my best wishes to your sister."

Shona nodded respectfully.

Annabelle stepped outside and began the long walk across the dark, open field toward her beloved blue Mini, guided by the flashing police lights and bright glow of the woods, her mind rolling with thoughts that were as lively as the young boy she had just left who was right now tossing in his bed trying to get to sleep.

Though Annabelle felt weary and ready for a good night's rest by the time she pulled into the yard that separated the church of Upton St. Mary and the small white cottage she called home, her mind was spinning with possibilities and theories.

She turned off the engine and stepped out of her car, bristling a little as a cold gust blew through her cassock. When she looked up, she noticed the small figure of Philippa, the church secretary, braving the wind as she ran with almost comically tiny steps toward the Reverend.

"Philippa! It's rather late for you to still be here, isn't it?"

Philippa clutched her coat around her as she drew close. "Hello, Reverend. I'm very sorry, but I was rather hoping you would give me a lift home. I completely lost track of time."

Though Annabelle was tired herself, she could never leave her most loyal friend to face the cool night alone. Philippa didn't live too far away, and in fact, it was a rather pleasant walk in the summertime. In unpredictable weather and cold snaps that emerged at other times of the year, however, it felt twice as long.

"Hop in," Annabelle said, with a good-natured shake of her head.

"Thank you, Annabelle," Philippa said, as she got in and placed her hands primly on her lap.

Annabelle reversed the car and pulled back out onto the country road.

"This is terribly unlike you, Philippa. Whatever were you doing that you lost track of the time?"

"Just my usual duties."

"Hmm," replied Annabelle, unconvinced, "you must have checked the accounting ledgers four times in the past week alone. And if you sweep those steps any more you'll wear them down to a ramp!"

"I'm just being thorough, Reverend."

Annabelle shook her head as she eased the car around the corners of the village's buildings.

"Believe it or not, yours isn't even the strangest behavior I've witnessed today. I'm beginning to wonder if there's something in the air."

Philippa remained silent.

Annabelle parked the car outside Philippa's well-maintained front garden and broke the silence with the click of her handbrake. Philippa promptly undid her seatbelt.

"Before you go," Annabelle said, turning in her seat to face her mousey friend, "I want to ask you something."

"Yes, Reverend?"

Annabelle frowned, seeking the right words. She didn't want to go spreading police business around – especially to someone as prone to gossip as Philippa – but she felt that she had to know more. And there was no better person to ask.

"Have you ever heard any rumors regarding a ghost in Upton St. Mary?"

Philippa's face stretched itself into an expression of such shock that all her wrinkles disappeared and she looked a full five years younger. She clasped a hand to her chest and stared at Annabelle as if she had transformed into a werewolf before her very own eyes.

"I... What.... Why would you ask me such a thing, Reverend?!"

Annabelle squinted at her colleague's overly dramatic reaction.

"Are you alright, Philippa?"

"Yes!" Philippa affirmed, sharply. "I'm absolutely perfectly fine! I just have no idea why you would ask me about a ghost!"

Annabelle opened her mouth to question Philippa's strange tone before thinking better of it. Philippa was a wonderful friend, but she had a habit of harnessing on to strange notions that caused her to act weirdly at times.

"Forget I asked. It was just a rumor I heard."

"What rumor?" Philippa blurted, almost before the Reverend had finished her sentence.

"Ah... Well..." Annabelle stuttered, suddenly feeling that she was the one put on the spot.

"Now you're the one acting strangely!" Philippa said triumphantly. She leaned forward, taking the initiative. "What's going on, Annabelle?"

"Nothing! Just... Well..."

For a few moments the two women exchanged odd looks with the rapidity of a tennis match, their expressions flickering between suspicious, annoyed, defensive, and frightened.

"Oh, this is ridiculous!" exclaimed Annabelle finally, throwing her hands in the air.

Philippa turned away, seeming relieved that whatever danger she had perceived from the Vicar's line of questioning was gone.

"Well, I'll see you tomorrow then, Philippa," Annabelle said, adding a shake of her head to her tone of defeat.

"Bye, Reverend," Philippa responded in a monotone as she got out of the car and made her way to her front door.

Annabelle watched her fumble for her keys and go inside before turning the car around and heading back to the church.

Ordinarily, Philippa's bizarre behavior would have been cause for concern enough. Today, it was just another strange event to add to the others. Almost everyone she had spoken to was exhibiting peculiar reactions, and Annabelle could not bear the feeling that she was standing on the edge of not just one, but several mysteries.

As a child, her father, a London cabbie who adhered to the profession's stereotype by having an opinion on everything, had a saying for certain kinds of drivers: 'They take a pound to start, and a pound to stop.' Annabelle felt that the saying could easily be applied to Upton St. Mary. A good event in the small village seemed to spark a snowball of positive feeling and good fortune that spread to everyone within its vicinity. Unfortunately, it worked the other way around too. If the behavior of DI Nicholls, Philippa, and Constable Raven were anything to go by, soon the whole village would be enraptured by the dark intrigue and paranoid speculation that seemed to be swirling around her.

She drove her Mini expertly along the winding roads. It was an experience that she usually savored as one of life's most underappreciated and satisfying pleasures. To drive along these elegantly arranged country lanes guided solely by the headlights of her car was, to her, heavenly. Tonight, however, it was a time of solitude and quiet during which her mind ran rampant with growing worries and concerns over the events of the day.

Top of the list had to be the identity of the body that young Dougie had discovered. Though she had become as much a staple of village life as the annual cake competition, Annabelle had only been in Upton St. Mary for a few years. Usually her closest friend would fill her in (a little too eagerly, and with a little more information than was strictly necessary) when she found her knowledge of Upton St. Mary's past, or its inhabitants, was lacking. But with Philippa acting in a manner that was so out of the ordinary, Annabelle would have to find another long-time resident and expert gossip to aid her in the investigation to find out who the body might be.

Of course, the question of whether Annabelle should even be getting involved with this police matter never occurred to her. She regarded the unveiling of the village's mysteries as part of her Godly duties. The maintaining of the villagers' peace of mind was a matter of course for the church vicar. That's how she saw it.

After all, it would by no means be the first time police work had overlapped with her churchly responsibilities and on those previous occasions her diligence, curiosity, and astute intuition had borne rather satisfying results. Already, she felt she had gained some insight that had not yet reached the admirable Inspector Nicholls: The ghost of Miss Montgomery's sister.

There's no way Dougie would have divulged play-ground hearsay to DI Nicholls. The Inspector was much too intimidating and abrupt for that. And even if he had, it's the sort of thing the detective would have dismissed out of hand even on his better days. Annabelle, however, was a strong believer that "out of the mouth of babes comes truth." A slightly distorted truth, perhaps, but a truth worth considering.

Just as she was engrossed in these deepest of thoughts, something darted across the road.

"Crikey!" Annabelle cried out, slamming on the brakes.

The car jolted to a halt, flinging Annabelle forward, then thumping her back against the seat. When she looked up again the road was empty. She had seen foxes cross the road before, and on one occasion a lone sheep, but this had looked more like a pig.

Surely not, thought Annabelle. Pigs were fenced in. They rarely roamed. She shook off the incident, too tired to add another question to her growing pile, and continued homewards.

When she reached the church, she parked her car beside her cottage and got out without taking a moment to appreciate the picturesque night sky as she usually did when arriving home at this hour. She entered her house in a hurry. She wanted to have a shower and get to bed; tomorrow was going to be a long and busy day. Especially if her instinct that this was only just the beginning of a period of complexity and intrigue turned out to be correct.

Dr. Robert Brownson could not stop fidgeting as he drove his white Honda Civic down the M3 toward Upton St. Mary. He alternated restlessly between having the radio on and turning it off, finding that his thoughts wandered out of control when it was off, and that most of the music reminded him of... her. At some point as he left behind the dense roads of London, he settled upon a talk radio station and decided to focus on the road that unfurled under the light of his car's headlamps. It was a long drive, made longer by his anticipation of what, and who, awaited him.

Ordinarily, he would not have driven throughout the night, but these were no ordinary circumstances. This was an opportunity that he felt compelled to grab with both hands, an opportunity that he had been waiting for for years, and one which he was most certainly not going to let pass through his fingers.

Dr. Brownson shuffled a little in his seat, finding that his most expensive suit had shrunk in the year since he had last worn it. He was successful, talented, and had established himself in the most privileged and distinguished circles of London's scientific community. However, there were few events in the calendar of a forensic anthropologist grand enough to demand his best clothes. This occasion was an exception.

The request had come through during the evening, much later than he typically received business calls. He had almost ignored it completely. The voice on the other end had been friendly but officious, a young police constable who requested his assistance on a case.

"Can't the local pathologist handle it?"

"She requested a forensic anthropologist. You, specifically."

At the mention of a female pathologist, Robert Brownson's thoughts were already in the past.

"Who requested me?" he asked, tentatively.

Upon hearing her name, Dr. Brownson was thrust sharply back into the past. A magical day at the Oxford Cambridge boat race. Punting down the River Cherwell. Passionate discussions about history and philosophy, where romance had blossomed across the overlap in their interests.

Robert Brownson had always been slightly shy, the kind of person who took time to reveal the full spectrum of his personality. He was humorous and good-natured, but he struggled to find opportunities where these positive qualities could flourish. At the time of his relationship with the raven-haired angel, he had felt blessed by her strong independence. Her incredible ambition and dedicated humility had given her, and indeed, those around her a sense of strength. He had felt emboldened. He could remember almost every conversation they had had, almost every item of clothing she had worn, and every which way she had styled her hair, like the notes to a song listened to many times over.

Unfortunately, the most vivid memory was that of her revelation. She would leave Oxford to take up a once-in-a-lifetime Ph.D. opportunity at a top university in America. There was nothing he could do or say. She was determined. He had been bereft.

Decades later, he was hearing her name again, associated with a case in a small village somewhere near the south coast of England. At times throughout the intervening years, he had teased and fortified himself with the notion that one day he would hear of her and descend to declare thirty years of pent-up feelings for the woman he had not stopped thinking about for the duration. But he knew it was not in his character. He would crumble before such a grand gesture.

Now though, years of good karma had been cashed in. He had been handed the greatest opportunity he would ever get – a coincidence so extraordinary it was enough to make a scientist believe in God – to reconnect with his one true love, the one that got away, his soulmate: Harper Jones.

CHAPTER THREE

ANNABELLE AWOKE FEELING breezy and light for about five seconds. After that, the concerns and questions that had troubled her during the previous day flooded her mind so vehemently that not even the dappled morning light could lift her spirits. She showered, dressed, and made her way into the kitchen, opening curtains as she passed through the house to let the morning sunshine infuse some of its uplifting energy into the rooms. As she was about to place some bread in the toaster, however, she heard a distant scratching sound coming from the church. She paused, listening closely. It stopped for a few moments, before starting up again with even more vigor.

"What on earth could that be at this time of morning?" she muttered to herself as she leaned across the sink to see out of the window.

Outside, wielding a broom as if it were a weapon was the small figure of Philippa, an expression of grim determination upon her face. Biscuit was watching from a tree branch and after a few moments, she leapt down and began eagerly chasing the broom that Philippa was sweeping briskly from side to side. Biscuit's "help" didn't seem to improve Philippa's mood any and she brushed the step even harder for a few moments before quickly prodding Biscuit, an action designed to deter the cat. An action that was successful.

"She brushed those steps yesterday!" Annabelle exclaimed to nobody in particular.

Philippa was by no means lazy, and indeed, seemed to take great satisfaction in undertaking the lion's share of the church's upkeep. It was just a little past eight on a Saturday morning, however, and combined with Philippa's lateness in leaving the church the day before, Annabelle began to grow deeply worried about her church secretary's behavior.

She rapped on the window loudly until Philippa, who was so engrossed in her task that it took her a while to notice, looked up. She locked eyes with the vicar and waved. Annabelle gestured for Philippa to join her in her cottage kitchen, and watched as the church secretary placed her broomstick aside almost reluctantly, before making her way over.

"Morning, Reverend," Philippa said quietly, as she stepped into the kitchen.

"How long have you been out there, Philippa?" Annabelle said, readying an extra cup for morning tea.

"Oh, not long," Philippa replied, "about an hour or so."

Annabelle decided to hide her surprise.

"Are you not sleeping well?"

"No, Reverend. I'm sleeping perfectly fine."

"Hmm," Annabelle concluded, unconvinced. "Toast?"

"Yes please, Reverend," Philippa answered politely. "I was in such a rush this morning that I didn't have any breakfast."

Annabelle turned her back to put some more bread in the toaster and to hide the look on her face. The mystery of what was troubling Philippa only seemed to grow more and more curious.

Once breakfast was ready, Annabelle placed the plates on the table and took a seat beside Philippa, who was eerily quiet for a woman who enjoyed passing judgment on all and sundry and rarely missed the opportunity to do so. They ate in silence for a while, to the music of crunched toast and cutlery clinking as they dug into scrambled eggs and bacon.

Annabelle mentally toyed with various questions that she could ask Philippa in order to probe further into what was bothering her but decided against it. Philippa knew Annabelle well enough to detect when she was fishing for information. Still, she was beginning to grow tired of feeling like there was much that she didn't know.

"I don't suppose you've heard any gossip coming from the village today, have you?" Annabelle asked, in as innocent and casual a manner as she could manage.

"No," Philippa said solemnly. "Though I'm to meet Barbara Simpson in a bit."

"Ah, Barbara! I've not seen her in a while."

"Vicars are rarely close with village pub owners," Philippa said, allowing herself the little witticism despite her quiet mood.

"Still, I'm long overdue on catching up with her," Annabelle said, warming to the idea.

"You're welcome to join us," Philippa said.

"And here she is," Annabelle exclaimed, looking out of the window as she jumped from her seat.

Sure enough, the buxom figure of Barbara Simpson, owner of the Dog And Duck, the most frequented pub in

Upton St. Mary, was tottering into the church driveway upon her high-heeled stilettos. Despite being barely five feet tall, Barbara Simpson was easy to recognize even at a distance, for the extravagant fake-fur coats she wore and her propensity for lurid, clashing colors. Though she was well into her fifties and undeniably one of the most astute and successful women in the village, Barbara possessed the taste in fashion of an adolescent schoolgirl. Her high-pitched, girlish voice seemed to reverberate for miles wherever she went while above her perpetually smiling face, heavily made-up in hues of pink (lips), red (cheeks), and blue (eyes), sat her proudest possession: her thick, pale-blonde hair, arranged into an elaborately sculpted beehive that she would caress and puff up frequently with her inch-long fingernails.

Annabelle opened her door and invited the woman inside.

"Thank you, Reverend! Ooh, it's been such a long time since I've been to church. I'm feeling all guilty!" she giggled, stepping into the kitchen and greeting Philippa.

"It's rather early for you, isn't it Barbara?" Annabelle said.

"Oh, I had to go to the market. Get the best veg for tonight's dinner menu before I was left with the scraps. Chef's off until lunchtime or he'd do it. I thought I'd have a chat with Philippa before going back to the pub."

"Would you like some tea?" Annabelle asked.

Barbara's larger-than-life face lit up as it did when she found something funny, which was rather often. "I always like it when I'm the one being offered a drink instead of the other way around. Especially when it's a vicar doing the asking!"

Annabelle smiled and got to work on the tea.

"How are you, my darling?" Barbara said to Philippa, placing an affectionate hand on her knee. "I've not seen you in days!"

"I've been a little busy at the church," said Philippa, smiling at her friend's concern.

"Well, you've missed out on all the juicy gossip! So much has been going on that even *I* can barely keep up with it!"

Annabelle placed Barbara's tea in front of her and sat down hopefully, ready to finally hear something that could give her a sense of what was happening.

"Thank you ever so much, Vicar. I know you don't drink, but if you ever fancy a good pot roast, it's on the house."

"Thank you, Barbara. You're always welcome to come to Sunday service yourself," Annabelle joked.

Barbara threw her head back and released her high-pitched giggle.

"You are a laugh, Vicar!"

"What's been going on?" Philippa asked uneasily, once the pub owner's laughter had died down.

"Well," Barbara began, leaning forward and taking on the low, astounded tone she usually used for dispensing gossip, "they found a body in the woods. A dead body. They've been running around all over the place to figure out what its doing there. They've even gone—"

Suddenly, Philippa stood up out of her seat, the squeak of the chair on the kitchen floor interrupting Barbara.

"Excuse me," Philippa said, her face pale, "I need to visit the little girls' room."

Annabelle and Barbara watched Philippa scurry out of the kitchen clutching a napkin to her face.

"Is there something wrong with Philippa?" Barbara

asked Annabelle, full of concern. "She looks like she's seen a ghost."

Annabelle shook her head regretfully.

"She's been acting strangely for a few days now. It's just one of the many mysteries that's cropped up lately."

"I hope she's alright," Barbara said, her brightly-painted lips pouting with worry.

"I don't know what the matter is. I would just avoid raising the subject of this body until she's feeling better."

"Right you are, Vicar," the blonde woman replied, nodding to confirm she understood.

"Actually," Annabelle began, leaning forward and lowering her voice, "there is something I would like to ask you. I had hoped Philippa would be able to help me, but as you can see, she's not very willing to discuss such things."

"Of course I'll help you. Ask away."

"It's about the body, actually. You've lived in Upton St. Mary for a long time, haven't you, Barbara?"

Barbara smiled. "Born and raised, Vicar! Though I always prefer telling people I've not been alive that long!"

Annabelle chuckled a little.

"Well, have you ever heard any rumors about Miss Montgomery the school teacher? Specifically her sister?"

Barbara's long, thick eyelashes splayed outward as she gasped her surprise. "You know what, I never thought of that! Yes, you're right, Vicar. That body could very well be her!"

"Who?" Annabelle said quickly, almost pleading for a name.

"Lucy. Louisa Montgomery's sister. I haven't thought about Lucy in years. I still see Louisa around sometimes though, carrying her huge carpet bag, as uptight as anything. She doesn't seem to have changed in – gosh –

twenty years, now? Lives just opposite Katie Flynn's tea shop – terrible fuss they had a while ago."

"Yes. But what about Lucy? Why did her sister disapp—"

Annabelle was so eager to blurt out her questions that she almost didn't notice Philippa's shuffling footsteps emerge from the bathroom. She stopped herself mid-sentence to smile at the small woman as she came back into the kitchen.

"Am I interrupting?" Philippa said quietly, almost hanging her head with embarrassment.

"Of course not!" Annabelle assured her, standing up from her seat. "I was just on my way out to perform some errands. I'll leave you two to yourselves."

"See you, Vicar."

"It was a pleasure catching up, Barbara. Hopefully I'll see you around."

"Likewise," Barbara said.

Philippa merely nodded, before sitting down and clasping her teacup with both hands in order to stop them from shaking.

Annabelle leaped into her Mini and started the engine. It roared into life eagerly, mirroring her mood that had been kick-started by the information she had just gleaned.

Barbara had not said much, indeed, she had been interrupted before fully embarking on her train of thought, but she had said enough. The teacher's name was Louisa Montgomery; her sister's name was Lucy. She lived opposite Katie Flynn's tea shop, a place that Annabelle knew well.

That was all Annabelle needed.

In all her time in Upton St. Mary, and of all the pieces of gossip she had come across, there was only one solution she knew would work when one wanted the truth and nothing but the truth: Go right to the source.

If there was any connection between that body in the woods and the alleged disappearance of Lucy Montgomery, she would find out from Louisa herself.

Even at this early hour, the village was bustling as it always was on Saturdays with the farmer's market at its center. Annabelle weaved her Mini through the rough, cobbled streets and turned the corner that led to Katie Flynn's tea shop.

The tea shop was situated on one of the most well-preserved, delightfully colorful, and sleepy – even by Upton St. Mary's standards – streets. What Annabelle found, however, as she drove her Mini carefully down its bumpy cobbles, was anything but calm.

"I saw you! That's not the way you hold a dog! If he wants to sniff the lamppost, you let him sniff the lamppost! Who do you think you are?" bellowed none other than DI Nicholls.

"I... I... I'm Terry Watson," stammered the frightened man who was cowering in the presence of the tall, imposing figure of the Inspector.

"I don't care what your name is! I don't care if you're the King of Egypt! When your dog wants to sniff something, you jolly well let him!"

Annabelle parked the car beside the two figures and jumped out of it.

"What's going on?" she said, walking up to the two men.

The Inspector turned to Annabelle and jabbed his finger toward Terry. "This man thinks it's okay to treat a dog as if it doesn't have feelings, as if it doesn't have instincts. He wants the dog to go against its very nature!"

"I do not!" Terry exclaimed, managing to muster enough courage to argue now that Annabelle was there.

"I bloody well saw you!" the Inspector roared. "What kind of man doesn't allow his dog to sniff a lamppost?! I've locked up hardened criminals more reasonable than you! This is animal cruelty! I've got half a mind to arrest you right now and stick you in a cell. Then you'll know what it's like to have somebody stopping you from doing what *you* want!"

"Stop it!" Annabelle shouted, firmly. "This is ludicrous. Terry loves his dog as well as if he were his own child. Why, Chester is one of the most well-behaved dogs in the county."

"Thank you, Annabelle."

"Are you taking his side?" Nicholls growled, his eyes wild.

"No!" Annabelle asserted. "Because there are no sides to take, Inspector. This is obviously a misunderstanding. Though I would expect better than berating a man on the street from an officer of the law!"

Terry shimmied slightly to the side as Annabelle and the Inspector locked gazes. With small steps, he shuffled away, and when he was certain that they hadn't noticed, he began walking briskly down the street, casting fearful glances behind him.

"Reverend," the Inspector began, some calm seeping into his voice, though he had a resolute expression on this face, "that was a police matter, one in which you had no business interfering."

Annabelle pursed her lips in frustration.

"I have every right to defend the respectability of people

living in my parish, Inspector. Especially when they are being subjected to the fury of a.... a... grump!"

The Inspector breathed heavily, blood dissipating from his cheeks as he slowly gathered his emotions.

"I have a deep respect for you, Reverend, but you can't tell me how to do my job."

Annabelle raised her chin.

"And how, Inspector, did your conversation with Louisa Montgomery go, exactly? You haven't been to see her already have you? You must have got her out of bed."

The Inspector's mouth opened in awe.

"How did you—"

"It's a fairly obvious connection to make, considering the body must have been in the woods for many years and her sister disappeared two decades ago. You certainly didn't come here to partake in the wonderful delicacies available at Flynn's tea shop or you would be a lot less abrasive. In fact, I would even surmise that your conversation with Louisa proved rather fruitless, considering the temper you just subjected that poor dog-walker to."

Annabelle watched as the Inspector mouthed the beginning of several words, before giving up entirely and bounding off down the street in a huff.

"This case won't go anywhere if you insist on being so hot-headed," Annabelle muttered to herself, as she watched him go.

She returned to her Mini, locked it, and strolled down the street. When she reached Flynn's tea shop, she examined the small house that was set a little way back from the road, directly opposite. It was rather less elegant than most houses in Upton St. Mary, though no less comfortable. Its well-trimmed hedges, crisply starched curtains, and buffed windows hinted at a houseproud, hard-working owner.

Annabelle took another step toward it before catching sight of something in the corner of her eye.

There were cupcakes with strawberry icing, a treat she had not enjoyed for some time. Éclairs with soft cream spilling out of them. A cheesecake set to the side topped with raspberries and blueberries. These visions seemed to permeate and gain control over her mind as they sat on sumptuous display in the window of Katie Flynn's tea shop. Momentarily forgetting the matter in hand, Annabelle entered a deep, hypnotic state from which she emerged to find herself, remarkably, standing at the tea shop counter speaking to Katie Flynn herself just a few seconds later.

"Hello, Reverend. The usual éclair?"

"Um... I think I'll try that cupcake, if I may. And a pot of Earl Grey, please."

"Absolutely. Take a seat, Reverend. I'll bring it over."

"Thank you, Katie."

Of course, Annabelle was still brimming with a sense of purpose and determination, but there was no harm in a little treat, surely?

She had decided to give Louisa a respite from visitors. If the Inspector had just been to see her, Annabelle would almost certainly be unwelcome, especially considering the Inspector's irritable mood. So she took a seat in the tea shop window that allowed her a full view of Louisa's home.

The cake and tea were brought over, and Annabelle savored every mouthful of the spongy, sugary, frosted confection. She washed it down with one cup of tea, and was just considering a second, when the door to the teacher's home opened. Annabelle leaned forward, focusing on the prim figure that diligently locked her front door and walked out to the street.

With her salt-and-pepper hair tied in a chignon at the

nape of her neck, and in a tweed skirt and jacket, a crisp white shirt complementing the ensemble, Miss Montgomery certainly appeared the part of a strict, spinster schoolteacher. She looked like she brooked no nonsense with the eight-year-olds she taught, particularly those as rambunctious as Dougie Dewar. Her signature look was completed, sure enough, by the large carpet bag she carried, the handles of which were looped over her forearm – just as Barbara had described.

Though she wore her hair in a severe style and had on only light-make up, her delicately featured face, with her strong cheekbones, supple skin, and mesmerizingly deep-green eyes, hinted at a once-great beauty. Her lovely features were not uplifted by an expression of goodwill or even good-naturedness, however, such was her downcast look. She looked at the ground as she hurried off.

In between bites of strawberry cupcake, Annabelle had been pondering whether she should actually speak to Louisa. The Inspector would no doubt have left a bad impression, and the subject of her sister may be a painful subject for Louisa. Annabelle waggled her head from side to side as she considered the pros and cons.

Still trapped in her indecision, Annabelle threw the last of her cupcake into her mouth, absent-mindedly stepping away from her table, through the door of the tea shop, and into the street. Soon she was following Louisa, hoping that she would get some sign that it might be possible to approach the teacher and get a reasonable reception.

Guiltily, Annabelle felt a certain glamour and excitement as she followed the woman through the quiet back streets of Upton St. Mary. She imagined herself one of the detectives she often saw in movies or on TV, secretly tracking their target to the source of the grand intrigue, though it was a little difficult to maintain necessary elusive, shadow-like qualities, due to the large black cassock she wore and the constant greetings she received from passers-by.

Annabelle was so engrossed in her private game of "chase" that she almost didn't notice the direction in which Louisa was heading. After five minutes it became clear that Louisa was not, in fact, shopping for groceries as Annabelle had thought. After ten, it was also apparent that she wasn't heading anywhere within the village, as she took a rarely-used path that led toward allotments that were situated on the fringes of Upton St. Mary.

Annabelle suddenly found herself sidling along hedgerows and hopping behind trees in order to remain out of sight as her quarry traversed the open fields beyond the path. Her playful "trailing" of the target had taken on a very ominous turn indeed.

Eventually, Louisa turned in toward a section of the allotments, balancing delicately on the grass corridors that crisscrossed between the vegetable plots. Annabelle hopped through some nettles, mouthed her frustration, and crouched behind a tree as she rubbed her stinging hands. In her ludicrous position, she was clearly visible to anybody passing by on the paths, and she prayed that she would not be required to explain herself. She peered around the oak tree trunk and watched as Louisa strolled up to a particularly beaten-looking shed and placed her carpet bag down carefully on the ground. Louisa unlocked the multiple padlocks which held the shed door shut, and went inside.

Annabelle watched the door close behind the teacher, and shuffled her feet as she tried to find a comfortable position in the nettles. She looked around and, mercifully, saw no one. How she would explain what a vicar was doing hiding behind a tree, in the midst of a patch of nettles, in the middle of a field, she had no idea. She kept her fingers crossed that her solitary status wouldn't change as, judging by the closed shed door, she was going to have to wait.

After about half an hour, Annabelle gave up all pretense of stealth. The excitement and thrill of the chase had evaporated, leaving her feeling ridiculous and in pain. Her crouching position had given her an incredible cramp, and each time she shuffled around to make herself more comfortable, she gathered another nasty sting on her hands, which were now red and swollen.

She had been lucky to not be seen from the path, but every additional minute was test of her fortune, and she had had about enough of this "game." With no sign that Louisa was about to emerge from her shed anytime soon, Annabelle stood up, brushed down her cassock, and dolefully limped back along the path, soothing her hands by rubbing them gently.

The lingering taste of strawberry cupcake, and her deep and sincere belief that she had earned another one, compelled her to return to Flynn's tea shop. As she opened the door once again, its sugary aroma struck her closely followed by an idea. She wondered briefly if the two were connected. Sugar. Idea.

Shaking her head, Annabelle returned to the matter in hand. Who better to ask about the enigmatic Louisa Montgomery than Katie Flynn, who no doubt saw the teacher frequently from across the street? Annabelle was also reminded of a remark that Barbara had made about some sort of "fuss" between the two. It was a perfect excuse for another cupcake.

"Hello again, Reverend," smiled Katie, with a wink. "Have you come in for another bite to eat?"

Annabelle chuckled. "You know me too well, Katie."

Katie laughed as she placed a cupcake on a plate and began fixing Annabelle more tea.

"Actually, Katie," Annabelle said, "do you have a moment to talk? I have something I'd rather like to ask you."

Katie looked around the tea shop, taking in the quiet atmosphere, then spoke to her niece and assistant, a wonderfully pretty girl who always had her head tucked into a book. "Sally? Would you mind taking care of any customers while I speak with the Reverend?"

Sally shrugged and nodded, before bowing her head once more into her paperback. Katie rolled her eyes, then walked with Annabelle to her table by the window.

"So, what's on your mind, Reverend?"

"Well, I was rather hoping to pick your brain about your neighbor across the road," Annabelle said, nodding toward Louisa's home.

"Oh," Katie said, her lips pursing disapprovingly, "I can tell you plenty about *her,* but it wouldn't be very neighborly."

Annabelle frowned with curiosity.

"I heard you had some fuss?"

"'Some fuss,' indeed, Reverend. If she had had her way, this place wouldn't even exist."

"The tea shop?"

"The very same," Katie said, nodding toward the strawberry cupcake between them.

"Why so?"

Katie looked across the road wistfully.

"It was a long time ago, but you don't forget that kind of thing. You see, I grew up here – in this very tea shop. It used to be our family home. Louisa," Katie said, almost struggling to say the name without grimacing, "and her family lived over there in that tiny house that Louisa now lives in by herself. So we sort of grew up together."

"You were friends?"

"Sure, I suppose," Katie said, reluctantly, after a moment's thought.

"What happened?" Annabelle asked earnestly, on the edge of her seat.

"About ten years ago, I married Tom Flynn – you know him. Well, when it came to deciding where we would live, it was an easy choice. Tom's house over on the hill was ten times the size of ours! As I was the eldest, and Harry – my brother – was away working in London, I didn't want to leave our family home empty."

"So you decided to turn it into a tea shop."

"And I've never looked back."

"It's the best in Cornwall."

Katie chuckled. "Thank you, Reverend. Certain people were against the idea from the start, however."

"Why?"

Katie shook her head in confusion. "I still don't really know. She said it would be 'noisy,' that it would 'ruin the aesthetics of the street,' that the house had been a home for years, and it would be a tragedy to change it into a business. At first I thought it was just the typical grumbles and resistance to change you hear at any old town hall meeting, but when she began getting lawyers involved, I got very upset indeed. They threw out her claims, of course, but it left a very bitter taste in my mouth – especially when the shop was supposed to bring pleasure, and tourists, to the whole village. Personally I think she's been a teacher for too long. She thinks she can boss around adults just as easily as she does her pupils!"

"It is rather strange."

"She's never been the same since her sister disappeared – not that she was so wonderful then, of course."

"Do you think her objections to the shop were about clinging to the past? Albeit in an odd way?"

Katie shrugged.

"Frankly, Reverend, I think you'd need more Godly forgiveness than I'm capable of to give her the benefit of the doubt to that extent."

Annabelle sighed sadly.

"Can you tell me anything about her sister? About how she disappeared?"

"Ah, you're going very far back there, Reverend. I can't even remember what I had for breakfast!"

"Please try."

Katie looked up and squinted as she brought forth memories long forgotten.

"Well, the one thing I do remember is that Lucy was as sweet as Louisa was sour. She was always smiling, always laughing. Everybody loved her. None of that intensity or aloofness that Louisa has. No, Lucy was an utterly lovely girl. I'm sure that's why they never got on."

"They argued?"

"No, nothing like that. They just... weren't like sisters at all. They never did anything together. Partly because Louisa always thought she was better than anyone else. If there was a school dance, you could be sure that Louisa wouldn't show up, and just as sure that Lucy would be the life of the party. If it was a nice day, you were sure to find Lucy skipping down the street to meet her friends, while

Louisa was locked up in her room with nothing but her books. I mean, put it this way, Reverend, you know almost every person in this village, and yet here you are, having to ask me about Louisa Montgomery. What does that say about her as a person?"

"Hmm," Annabelle murmured, "I suppose you have a point."

"Oh! And she was so disapproving of Lucy having a boyfriend. You'd think she was her mother, rather than her older sister! The crazy thing was that Louisa herself had a boyfriend! If that's not the definition of hypocrisy then I don't know what is!"

"So she was protective of Lucy?"

"Bah!" Katie said, brushing the idea aside. "If you're looking for good intentions from Louisa Montgomery, you'll need to dig very deep. If you ask me, Louisa was jealous of Lucy. Lucy was younger, prettier, more popular, and had the entire world at her feet. Most people would be proud to call Lucy their sister. Louisa was simply proud."

Annabelle thought over what Katie was saying as she took a large bite of her cupcake and followed it up with some sips of piping hot tea. She placed the cup down gently and looked once more at the tea shop owner.

"How did Lucy disappear?"

Katie looked once again into the distance, her mind diving into the depths of her memories.

"It was about twenty years ago, now. I believe she had gone out with her boyfriend, and she just vanished. Never came home."

"Did they question the boyfriend?"

"I believe they did," Katie said, the slowness of her words and the troubled look in her eyes indicating that she was at the limits of what her memory could bring forth, "but they never arrested him. I think he had an alibi, or perhaps there was some confusion over exactly when it happened."

"It's all very curious."

"Oh," Katie said adamantly, "I remember the impact it had very well. The whole village was stunned. Lucy was a friend to everyone, her loss affected all of us. Some people were angry, some wouldn't let it go, and most of us were extremely sad. It was a very dark time."

"For Louisa, too?"

"Yeah," Katie said, "even for her. If she was prickly previously, she was positively reclusive after the incident. You'd get an occasional 'hello,' or a simple conversation out of her before her sister disappeared, but when she lost her sister, she gave up on other people completely."

"That's a terrible story," Annabelle said.

"Yes, it is," Katie agreed. "It takes a long time for such wounds to heal."

"For some people those kinds of wounds never fully do," Annabelle replied.

Katie nodded.

"Do you remember who Lucy's boyfriend was?"

Katie once again peered into the distance, lines of deep concentration forming around her eyes.

"You know, I really don't. My memory is fuzzy. I could tell you a dozen names, but I wouldn't be sure about any of them!" she laughed.

"That's alright," Annabelle said. "Twenty years is a long time. I doubt I could remember much of what I was doing twenty years ago."

"It's like I say, Reverend, you remember the things that change your life."

"That's very true, Katie."

"How come you're so interested in this, Reverend? Has Philippa been regaling you with stories from the past?"

Annabelle smiled. "No, Philippa's been rather introspective herself, lately. Actually, I'm surprised you haven't heard the news yourself, Katie. I'm under strict orders not to tell anyone."

"Oh, come now, Reverend! Surely I deserve something in return for my history lesson!"

Annabelle chuckled.

"You'll probably hear it soon anyway. This business with Louisa's sister is about to become the talk of the town once again."

Katie's face dropped.

"What do you mean?"

"They found a body in the woods last night."

"Lucy's?!"

Annabelle shrugged.

"From what you tell me, Katie, I don't see who else it could be."

CHAPTER FOUR

D R. BROWNSON'S FOOTSTEPS echoed ominously around the clean, hard walls of the hospital. There were few people around at this time of the morning, his only interactions being with the receptionist who indicated in which direction he would find the morgue and the cleaner who nodded a perfunctory greeting.

He walked slowly and steadily, his bearing almost regal. He felt like a man about to meet his fate, a prince about to take the crown, an athlete about to ascend the podium. He distracted himself from his jangling nerves by fidgeting with the bouquet of roses he carried delicately in his clammy palm, and brushing the sides of his grey-brown curls, occasionally checking his reflection in a well-polished window to make sure he hadn't brushed his hair too much. The large double doors loomed at the end of the corridor like the gates to heaven, and his heart raced ever more quickly as he made his way forward, step by step.

Robert Brownson was suddenly struck by a thought that seared through him with the power of a lightning bolt:

Would Harper Jones still remember him? He stopped in his tracks, his mouth open with shock. After a moment to gather his senses, he realized the stupidity of the thought – Harper Jones had been the one who asked for him! He smiled to himself, shook his head, and slowly began walking again.

After another few steps he froze once more. What would he say? It had been so long. He vividly remembered Harper's keen gaze, her brevity with words, and her ability to make others feel like they were in the spotlight. When they were younger, he had often struggled to say the right thing to her. Now that they had not spoken for so long, he had even less of an idea of what to say. What if she had not lost that focused, silent intensity, just as he had not lost his bumbling clumsiness when it came to conversation?

Brownson took out the white handkerchief he had spent over five minutes neatly folding into his pocket, adjusting it to be as precise and as neat as Harper herself, and wiped it across his brow. He was sweating and suddenly felt immensely claustrophobic in the hospital hallway. He caught sight of a water cooler some way down another corridor and hurried toward it. The glug of the water echoed against the walls as he filled paper cup after paper cup and downed them one after the other.

He breathed deeply, feeling both calmer and cooler.

For goodness sake, Robert! he thought to himself. *You're a man of over fifty! You can't be nervous at the prospect of meeting a colleague!*

After preparing himself with these words, however unconvinced of them he really was, he threw the paper cup into the nearby bin, picked up the bouquet once again, stiffened his back, and marched toward the doors marked 'morgue.'

As soon as he entered the room, however, whatever romantic scene Dr. Brownson had imagined previously disappeared entirely, as half a dozen people of various ages and sizes, all clothed in white coats, spun their heads and caught sight of him standing there with the bouquet in front of him like a knight preparing to joust.

Up until now, Brownson had imagined his meeting with Harper as intimate, the two of them greeting in a warm, friendly manner among the scientific paraphernalia they had once spent so much time with. In his daydreams, he had seen them leaning over some wonderful artifact, enthralled by a particular aspect of it as much as by each other's company, two dedicated scientists indulging their similarly potent passions for enlightened thinking.

Instead, the morgue was bustling with movement and the clinking of equipment – at least, until he walked in. The people in white coats were all moving around a table at the center of the room, the bones lying upon it anything but wonderful. Dirt, greenery, and pebbles were in the process of being cleaned from them, the messy debris providing a stark contrast to the sterile mortuary. The decomposed figure laid out looked almost terrifying and even at his distracted first glance, Dr. Brownson could tell that this skeleton had a rather sad story to tell.

"Ah..." he stammered, taken aback by the sheer number of people looking at him, as well as the clinical, deathly atmosphere that befell the room and the shattering of his fantasies. He glanced at the roses in his hand, looking at them as if they had been placed there by someone else, then tossed them aside onto a counter, causing instruments to clang to the floor. Everyone stared at him as the last vibrato tone of a pair of fallen tongs preceded complete and utter silence.

Just as Dr. Brownson was about to make his apologies and scurry out of the hospital, into his car, and back to his home in London, the figure at the head of the table took off her glasses and smiled.

"Robert!"

It was Harper. As radiant as ever. Still impossibly beautiful and almost magically youthful. So startling was she that Brownson almost believed her to be somebody else. She looked a full two decades younger than her forty-eight years. The bright sparkle of her green eyes and wide lips which seemed to save all their light for rare, powerful smiles were unmistakable, however.

Dr. Brownson's earlier embarrassment disappeared along with his awareness of the rest of the room, as his eyes focused only upon Harper making her way toward him and taking his arm. Suddenly, he felt as if he were an audience in his own mind, unable to believe this was really happening, watching what unfolded as though it was happening to somebody else.

"Everyone," Harper called to the rest of the team, "this is Dr. Robert Brownson, the finest forensic anthropologist in England. Robert, this is a small team of people I've brought in to help. They're mostly medical students and assistants who will cater to your every whim. Whatever you wish for, they shall divine."

The team nodded respectfully, a few of them uttering courteous 'hellos,' though Dr. Brownson's eyes were fixed upon the transcendent figure next to him.

"Harper!" he managed to say, as she led him toward the table. "How are you? Why, you look as wonderf—"

"So as you can see, the bones have been underground long enough that roots have formed between them. I'm no botanist, but it seems to me that an estimate of…"

Brownson gazed into her face, her words growing ever more incomprehensible and elusive to follow. Try as he might to concentrate upon what she was saying, the sound of her voice captivated him so intensely that he struggled to focus on the meaning of her words. He basked in the music and the rhythm of her exquisite voice, vowels pitched in the most heavenly keys possible, consonants so expertly and delicately uttered. He felt himself carried away on a soft pillow of sound he had almost forgotten.

"...though in my personal opinion the femur indicates an age of mid to late-teens, what do you think?"

Brownson's eyes were closed, but after a few moments he noticed that the beautiful sound of Harper's voice had disappeared, and he re-opened them.

"Robert?" Harper repeated, the anthropologist's silence catching the attention of several team members who shot surprised glances at Harper.

"Ah... Yes... Sorry."

Harper looked at Dr. Brownson with a furrow in her brow.

"Let me see," he said, buying himself time to gather his senses by peering at the bones in front of him.

Harper leaned down and spoke into his ear.

"Are you quite alright, Robert? Do you need some rest before we start? You've been driving all night."

"No, no, I shall be fine. Your smile has infused me with an energy no amount of sleep could replicate," he whispered.

Harper looked at Brownson and squinted suspiciously. The group that had by now all gathered around the body shuffled awkwardly before observing the anthropologist keenly as he resumed probing and poking absently at the skeleton.

"So what do you think, Dr. Brownson?" one of the assistants piped up.

"Do you remember," Dr. Brownson ignored his inquisitor, and began to speak again to Harper, his mind far too captivated by his thoughts to concentrate upon his work, "when we took a trip to Brighton Beach? We went in the water, but you were so concerned about your hair that you would only go up to your waist!"

Brownson laughed heartily, causing a few more members to cast confused expressions toward him.

"Um..." Harper said, clearing her throat. "Yes. I was just wondering, however, what age you would place the body based on the—"

"Of course, of course," Dr. Brownson said, turning his head once more to the collection of bones. He prodded a little more but when everyone had turned their attention once again to the skeleton on the table, Dr. Brownson leaned in toward Harper again, a warm smile upon his face.

"I must say," he whispered, as his hands continued to work a particularly tough particle of dirt away from one of the bones, "you don't look a day older than the last time I saw you. It's simply remarkable."

Harper smiled neatly, though there was a certain amount of tension around her jaw. She looked straight at him and indicated with her eyes for him to focus on the bones. "Thank you. That's nice of you to say. You look very well yourself, Robert."

Dr. Brownson smiled warmly and cast his eyes around the table at the assistants who returned his inexplicable grin politely. He continued to work on the bones, grasping at a nearby brush in order to get a better look at a cavity.

"Canst thou O cruel, say I love thee not, when I against my self with thee partake?" he said.

"Ah… Dr. Brownson."

"Do I not think on thee when I forgot, am of my self, all-tyrant, for thy sake?"

"Doctor…"

"That was one of your favorite sonnets, do you remember?" Dr. Brownson said, with glee, all attempts at discretion now discarded. "I would read you a different one each time we parted. That particular one was when—"

Dr. Brownson felt firm fingers grip his forearm and pull him toward the morgue entrance. Harper wrenched the door open and yanked the doctor outside with an ease that suggested remarkable strength for such a slight woman.

He looked around him, as if stunned to find himself outside, before settling his eyes once again on Harper and smiling as if he realized her intentions.

"What is the matter with you? This is neither the time nor the place, Robert," said Harper, her voice firm and resolute.

"You're right," replied Dr. Brownson, standing upright. "I'm sorry. I just got carried away."

"I have a team in there, hadn't you noticed?" continued Harper. "They expected an experienced forensic anthropologist…not a Shakespeare-quoting, sonnet-serenading poet!"

Dr. Brownson nodded apologetically. "You're right. I'm being terribly unprofessional. It's just that it's been so long since I've seen you, and it's stirring so many pleasant memories!"

Harper sighed.

"Let's get back in there and do our work," Dr. Brownson said, wearing a pleased smile, "and as soon as we're done, I would be honored if you would join me for dinner, I mean, breakfast. We'll catch up – we've got decades to get through after all!"

Dr. Brownson chuckled and stepped toward the door, but a strong grip pulled him back once again. When his eyes met Harper's, his face dropped.

"Robert..."

"Don't look so shocked! I know it's been a long time, but just looking at you I can see you've not changed very much at all. As for me, well, I'm pretty much the same man you knew at Oxford! I daresay it'll be just as if you never left!"

"Robert... Are you implying what I think you're implying?"

Dr. Brownson smiled and nodded happily.

"Yes, Harper. Though it's been over twenty years, my feelings haven't changed one bit."

She looked up at him sorrowfully, her eyes full of pity. She raised her hand for Dr. Brownson to see the large emerald ring on her third finger.

"I'm married, Robert. I have been for many years now. I'm sorry if you thought this was anything more than a professional consultation."

Dr. Brownson opened his mouth but found himself empty of words. Once again he felt as if the hospital walls were constricting him, causing his brow to sweat and a slight feeling of nausea to well up inside of him. He gulped loudly, his mouth dry, and stammered.

"Ah...Well..."

"I'm sorry, this," she nodded at the morgue entrance, "was insensitive of me. I should have met with you first. Privately." Robert looked down at the floor.

"If you prefer," continued Harper, her voice exhibiting a gentleness she was unused to showing, "I can arrange for another forensic anthropologist. Dr. Livingstone lives only a few mi–"

"Ha," Dr. Brownson said, with unconvincing joviality,

"Livingstone is a hack. He couldn't distinguish a homo sapiens from a homophone."

They smiled at each other, though Harper couldn't help noticing the pained look in Dr. Brownson's eyes. He took a deep breath, shuffling his feet and smoothing his clothes briskly, feeling ever more lost under the gaze of the woman he loved.

"Married. Of course. Why wouldn't you be? Sorry. Got it wrong, obviously. You know me, imagination like a unicorn – fantastical! Never was good with people – give me some dusty, dry old bones any day!"

Harper smiled sweetly, hoping it would soothe Dr. Brownson's embarrassment and hurt feelings, but the beauty of it only made his pining more sorrowful. Somehow, he managed to force a little laugh which sounded shallow in the long echoing emptiness of the hospital hallway.

"Perhaps you should go home, Robert."

"No, no, it's okay," he said, after a few deep breaths. "There's only really one thing that will take my mind off this, and that's work. Lead the way, Dr. Jones."

Harper led Dr. Brownson back into the morgue. There were a few snickers and giggles, but Harper quickly stared those down. She stood beside the cranium on the table and was joined by Dr. Brownson.

"So what do you estimate for an age?"

"Fifteen, sixteen. Certainly fits the profile of a girl that age," Dr. Brownson said, briskly. "The bone remodeling on the hips hasn't deteriorated much. That, combined with the fully–grown tibia makes it a near certainty."

A few of the younger team members gathered around the table, still smiling at the doctor's earlier antics. Harper cast them a steely look to remind them that mockery would not be tolerated.

"This damage to the cranial cavity is very interesting."

"We thought so too," piped up a rather confident young male assistant. "But there was a tree root grown through it. Because of that, we thought the damage to the skull likely occurred after death, posthumously."

Dr. Brownson glanced quickly at the assistant.

"The root that went through the bottom of her skull?"

The assistant nodded, smiling.

"That's a rather long leap of logic. You assume a root that was weak enough to go around the jawline, was suddenly strong enough to burst through the cranium? I have to disagree with your conclusion there, young man. This cranium was crushed *before* the root began growing through it. The damage may have increased, but if you look at the skull in profile, you can clearly see how it has been altered by a blow."

The young man shared an abashed glance with his equally-young neighbor, his earlier silent mockery of Dr. Brownson quickly dissipating in the face of his humiliation.

"This is strange," Dr. Brownson said, as he probed inside the skull. Slowly, he pulled out a wrinkly object from its center: A shriveled apple.

"Wow!" came a voice from one of the assembled team members. "How did that get there?"

Dr. Brownson shook his head. "These entire remains present a box of mysteries. Look at these fractures along the arms and legs. They're small, but they were undoubtedly created during this person's lifetime. If you look closely," he said, leaning to inspect the bones and rub away some of the dirt, "you can even find evidence of healing. This kind of healing occurs in childhood."

"What does it mean?" the young man asked again, his cockiness giving way to genuine curiosity.

"This person was beaten throughout her lifetime. Since childhood, in fact. I'd even posit that the beatings increased in severity. She was a healthy person so they may not have been obvious, and they quickly healed, but they were severe nonetheless."

"That's horrendous!" came a voice from around the table again.

"Indeed," replied Dr. Brownson.

"And the apple?" asked the young man, respect for Dr. Brownson now having replaced his earlier ridicule.

Dr. Brownson shrugged. "It would have decomposed by now if it were placed inside the skull at the time of death so I think we can conclude it is a relatively recent addition to the crime scene. I imagine the body was found in a rather shallow grave, yes?"

Harper nodded.

"It's possible that the apple was put there by someone or merely discarded close by and happened to find its way into the skull cavity, perhaps carried there by an animal. A bizarre coincidence, if that is the case."

Lulled by the warm, inviting atmosphere of the tea shop, and pondering over the elaborate picture of the past that Katie Flynn had just painted for her, Annabelle had spent the past thirty minutes gazing out of the window, deep in thought. Deciding that she should give herself some respite from her reflections on disturbing village events, she picked up a local newspaper from the counter and decided to peruse the lighter, more entertaining sections.

She took a final bite of her cheesecake (which had appeared at her table after she had dispatched the last of her cupcake as if by magic, so little did she remember ordering it), and feeling rather full, she smiled as she read the story of a young boy from Upton St. Mary who had just returned from a trip to the North Pole. She looked up, hoping to find another tea shop customer with whom she could coo over the brave young man, when a stern, familiar figure across the street caught her eye. Louisa Montgomery.

Sure enough, Louisa must have attended to her shopping after that mysterious business in her allotment shed, for her carpet bag was so full that it weighed the teacher down and dramatically slowed her pace. Leeks, bread, and cucumbers were peering precariously over the bag's rim.

Annabelle hurriedly popped the last raspberry from her cheesecake into her mouth and bustled toward the counter to pay her bill. As soon as she was done, she opened the tea shop door, the bell above it tinkling as she did so. She walked quickly across the street, glad of fresh air and exercise with which to assuage her guilty feelings for being a "little piggy" as her mother used to say.

"Miss Montgomery!" cried Annabelle, cheerily.

At the sound of her name, Louisa spun around so quickly that the cucumber that had been trying to escape from her bag finally made it. It dropped to the ground, bounced once, and began to roll into the road. Louisa quickly leaned forward to pick up the errant vegetable, completely forgetting about the others that were on the edge of jumping ship, too. Three oranges, two apples, and a grimy-looking cabbage were soon rolling away in different directions as Louisa wrestled with her bag to stifle any more escapees.

"Oh gosh!" Annabelle exclaimed, as she quickly darted

around the teacher, picking the food items up. "I'm sorry. I didn't mean to startle you."

"Hmph," grunted Miss Montgomery, her condescending gaze and the barely perceptible shake of her head saying everything her words were not. Annabelle was suddenly all too aware of what Katie had meant when she said that Louisa spoke to everybody as if they were children.

"There you go," Annabelle said, tucking the veggies back into Louisa's bag. Louisa snatched the remaining cucumber from Annabelle's hands and placed it in the bag herself.

"Thank you," she said, with great difficulty. "But I do not need your help. I do not intend to attend church anytime soon."

Annabelle, once she had recovered from Miss Montgomery's startlingly curt tone, said, "I do apologize. I was only trying to be helpful."

"If you wish to be helpful, then do not call my name so rudely when I am carrying my shopping."

Annabelle watched as Louisa continued to jostle the food, forcing it deeper into her bag insistently. She could see that Louisa was in no mood to talk so turned away and took a few steps down the street before changing her mind and circling back.

"I only wished to advise you, Miss Montgomery, that it would be a good idea to assist the police in their investigation into your sister's disappearance."

The close attention Miss Montgomery had been paying to securing the vegetables in her bag was suddenly replaced with a look of astonishment that she shot toward the Vicar. Annabelle held her gaze, waiting for Louisa to take the next step.

After looking up and down the road and swallowing,

Louisa gestured for Annabelle to walk up the path to her house.

"Please come in, Reverend."

Annabelle duly obliged.

Louisa unlocked her door and stepped inside. She was shaking as Annabelle followed her. As soon as Annabelle had passed into the hallway, Louisa quickly shut the door and addressed her visitor.

"How do you know? The Inspector insisted that nobody knew about this."

"Actually, it seems like most people in the village are aware of the new developments in your sister's case – more so than me. As for the body found in the woods, I witnessed the scene myself last night."

"It can't be my sister," Louisa said, as if to herself.

Annabelle hung her head solemnly.

"The body was... It's been there for a long time."

"That doesn't mean anything."

"Maybe we should sit down and talk about this."

"What is there to talk about?!" Louisa cried, desperation suddenly sparking fiercely in her eyes. "My sister is gone! That's it! Talking won't bring her back!"

Louisa grabbed her bag in frustration and marched into her kitchen, where she angrily began unpacking her groceries. Annabelle turned to the door, then back to the kitchen, wondering what she should do. The teacher seemed entirely unable to discuss anything right now, let alone the matter of her sister's death, but Annabelle was certain that such an opportunity would not present itself again. Slowly, she inched forward into the kitchen, where she saw Miss Montgomery grabbing and stacking groceries with alarming fury.

She watched for a few moments, searching her mind for

words that would both calm the angry woman and encourage her to reveal something pertinent. Sensing her presence, Louisa spun around to face Annabelle, a bunch of carrots in her hand, clutched as forcefully as a weapon.

"There is simply no use in digging up the past. What's done is done. I don't see why it's anybody's business but my own."

"I understand," Annabelle said sympathetically, stepping forward. "But there will be a police investigation. They will most likely reopen the case now they have new evidence."

"If they could have found out who did it, they would have found out back then!" Louisa said in a pleading voice. "This will achieve nothing!"

"But don't you want to know who did this?"

Louisa seemed to crumble, falling into a chair like a puppet whose strings had been cut.

"I don't care who did it," she said, mournfully, "I just don't want to deal with all the gossip again. The half-truths, the wild stories, the speculation. About my sister. About me. About Daniel."

"Daniel?" Annabelle said, quickly.

"Her boyfriend," Louisa said, softly, before adding, "at the time."

Annabelle mused over the name for a few seconds.

"Was he suspected of having something to do with her disappearance?"

Louisa closed her eyes and nodded slowly.

"What happened to him?"

Louisa – her eyes still closed – merely shrugged.

Taking note of Louisa's growing reluctance to talk about Daniel, Annabelle decided to change tack.

"You had a boyfriend at the time too, didn't you?"

Louisa looked at Annabelle, her eyes hardening. "I did."

"Wh... What happened?" Annabelle asked, as gently as she could, hoping that Louisa would not have another outburst.

Instead, Louisa snorted derisively.

"We got married. And then we got divorced."

"Why?" asked Annabelle again, feeling she were pushing her luck somewhat.

She watched Louisa stare into the distance, silent and contemplative. Just as Annabelle was sure that Louisa had not heard the question or simply would not answer it, she said:

"Because I didn't love him."

Annabelle felt like she was about to burst, she was so full of questions and curiosity. Louisa Montgomery had turned out to be a fascinating figure, both brusque and rude, yet vulnerable and hurt. Annabelle left her sitting alone, staring out of the window, no doubt burrowing deep into her past where her memories and reflections would only bring her pain.

Annabelle jumped into her car and drove away from the village center, turning over each word of Louisa's conversation in her mind as she searched for clues. Not that she needed to, because she had already received the biggest one yet – Daniel, Lucy's boyfriend.

Something about the way Louisa had spoken his name had resonated in Annabelle's mind. She had spoken it with the same warmth that she had spoken about her sister. Annabelle was in no doubt that Daniel was an integral part of this story. She had to find him.

Annabelle knew plenty of Daniels. Daniel was a

popular name in the village and surrounding area, from Terry the dog-walker's quiet, well-spoken nephew, Daniel Robbins, to Daniel Holden, the village's only war veteran.

Of course, it was entirely possible, perhaps even likely, that Lucy's boyfriend had left Upton St. Mary after the macabre incident, but it was still worth investigating. People who grew up in the village tended to return frequently, its idyllic vistas and strong sense of community a rarity elsewhere in the world.

Annabelle was proud of her ability to commit the contacts in her address book to memory, and she was still mentally flicking through its pages when she parked the car in the churchyard. She hopped out of her car and walked to the door at the back of the church.

"...Daniel Jones, the pharmacist – but he moved here shortly before me. Then there's Daniella Watson – of course not. Daniel... Daniel.... Dani–"

"Eeeeek!" came a shriek, as Annabelle turned a corner in the passage to her office and bumped into something small and hard.

Philippa spun around, saw Annabelle, and screamed again. "Aaaaaah!"

"Philippa!" Annabelle shouted, her face twisting into a look of sheer horror and confusion. "What's wrong?!"

"Oh, Reverend," Philippa said, immediately calming down. She was clutching at her chest with one hand and rubbing her cheek with the other. "It's you."

"Of course, it's me!" Annabelle said, still filled with astonishment at her church secretary's reaction. "Who else would it be?!"

Philippa shook her head and turned back to her work, anxiously sifting through prayer books. "Never mind."

Annabelle put her hands on her hips and frowned.

"That's enough, Philippa. This has gone far beyond ridiculous. I demand that you tell me what it is that's troubling you, this instant."

Philippa once again shook her head, quietly counting the prayer books out to herself.

"Philippa," Annabelle continued sternly, "if you do not tell me what is wrong, then I will regard it as the height of rudeness."

Philippa slowly counted out one more prayer book, then turned to face Annabelle with a look of deep reluctance.

"I'm sorry, Reverend. I would like to tell you, but it's not something that can be spoken of in a house of God – nor to a person of the cloth."

Annabelle's eyes widened.

"Don't be silly, Philippa. You're just making me even more determined to find out what it is you are hiding! What would make you say such a thing?"

"I'm sorry, Annabelle."

"Well, if you insist on not telling me, then I'll just have to guess."

"Please don't."

"Let's see now," hummed Annabelle, placing a finger upon her lips and looking up, "what could be so embarrassing that you wouldn't even say it to a priest..."

"I'd rather not–"

"I've got it. It's those scratch cards, isn't it? You've developed an addiction to them, and you're worried about how sinful it is."

"No!" Philippa said, appalled at the accusation. "I've not committed any sin! Well, none that I'm terribly ashamed of."

Annabelle smiled.

"Okay. So what is it, then?"

Philippa shifted her weight from one foot to the other, looking around her as if hoping for some escape route that would lead her away from the Reverend's line of inquiry. When she realized that she was well and truly trapped, she spoke reticently.

"I... I saw something."

Annabelle knit her brow.

"What?"

"That's all I'm going to say, Reverend. Please, don't ask me any more," Philippa begged, before turning back to the prayer books and beginning her count from the beginning.

Annabelle gave her friend one last sympathetic purse of the lips before resting her questions. She already had more than one mystery tugging at her capacities. She would have to be patient regarding Philippa's.

CHAPTER FIVE

AS IT APPEARED to be one of the last days of
the year that the sun was going to be generous
with its warmth, Annabelle sat with a mug of tea
on the bench that overlooked the cemetery behind St.
Mary's church. With a large ringed notebook on her knee, a
cup of tea steaming beside her, and a pen she twirled and
tapped against her lips, Annabelle intended to conceive the
Sunday sermon she would have to perform tomorrow, as
well as come up with some ideas for the autumnal events
the church had in its calendar.

She gazed out beyond the thick, aged stones that
comprised the wall that surrounded part of the churchyard
and looked toward the rolling hills that extended far into the
turquoise sky. She tried to keep her thoughts focused. Somewhere on the horizon, she noticed a figure rising slowly and
purposefully up one of the largest hills, before perching on
its crest and unloading what seemed like a square board
from a bag. She squinted and peered keenly, hoping to
discern what the person was doing, before another form
toward the bottom of the hill caught her eye. It looked like it

was a four-legged animal, rapidly moving across the fields with a clumsy gait and a confused, lost air about it.

The sound of crunching footsteps behind her pulled her attention away from the surprisingly busy scene on the hillside and she turned to look in their direction.

"I've brought you some biscuits, Reverend," Philippa said, holding out a plate of chocolate shortbread.

"Oh, these will hit the spot!" Annabelle said, glad of the interruption.

Philippa placed the plate beside Annabelle's tea, nodded formally, and turned back toward the church. From the corner of her eye, Annabelle noticed the church cat, Biscuit, silently making her way around the back of the bench. Annabelle pulled the plate of shortbread closer toward her to thwart the greedy tabby's thieving intent.

"Philippa! I had hoped you would keep me company. I have something I rather want to ask you."

Philippa turned around slowly, seeming to look for an excuse, and then reluctantly sat down.

"Reverend, I'd really rather not talk about—"

"Oh, tosh. I didn't mean that," Annabelle said, reassuringly.

Philippa seemed to relax and she turned her head inquisitively, inviting Annabelle to speak her mind.

"Do you happen to know any Daniels in the village?"

Philippa tilted her head away for just a moment to think, before turning back to Annabelle and saying, "To be perfectly honest, Reverend, I can think of quite a few."

Annabelle nodded. "I believe the one I am looking for is in his late-thirties. I'm not even sure he is even still *in* the village, but I know with some certainty that he was here roughly twenty years ago."

Philippa looked to the ground as she mentally sifted

through the ample list of people she knew. Annabelle watched her, patiently waiting for her reply.

"The only person I can think of that fits that description is Daniel Green, the butcher. Daniel Thompson is in his forties, but he only moved here a decade ago. Daniel Smalling has lived here all his life, all sixty years of it. There's Daniel Bennett, but he's only seven. No, Daniel Green is the only one I can think of who is in his late thirties and grew up here."

Annabelle bit into the end of her pen as she considered Philippa's words.

"I don't believe I've ever had the pleasure of Daniel Green's acquaintance."

"Oh, but you've most certainly had the pleasure of his meat, Reverend. Green's Butchers are renowned all over Upton St. Mary and beyond. His smoked cuts caused a sensation during last year's farmers' fair, don't you remember?"

"Hmm," Annabelle said, "I remember hearing something to that effect. Though as someone who'd munch her way through a chocolate log over a chicken leg, I can see why I'd never have met him."

"He slaughters the animals himself. It's the freshest meat you'll find in Cornwall," Philippa said, livening up at the chance of indulging in some gossip, however mundane, "and he's turned it into a very tidy business for himself. He's not bad looking either, and he's single!"

"I hope you're not implying what I think you are," Annabelle said, with a note of humor.

"Implying?" Philippa said, failing to hide her wry smirk. "I'm just saying he's one of Upton St. Mary's most eligible bachelors. He'll make a woman very happy one day – especially if she likes to eat well."

"Philippa!" Annabelle said with mock anger, before laughing good-naturedly. She considered whether she should probe Philippa as to the relationship Daniel had had with Lucy Montgomery, but she was afraid it would ignite another bout of paranoid nervousness and decided against it. It was nice to see her friend smile again and she didn't want to break her good mood. It had been rather a long time.

"Sorry, Reverend. Why do you ask?"

"I must speak with him about something."

"You can usually find him at his butcher's shop, he's often out the back."

"Right," Annabelle said, standing up and tucking her notepad and pen into her cassock, "I'll go find him right away." Then she noticed the plate Philippa had placed between them on the bench and sat down abruptly once again. "Right after I taste these shortbread biscuits," she added, biting into one almost before she had finished the sentence.

Philippa certainly wasn't overstating the point about it being a thriving business, thought Annabelle as she arrived outside Green's Butchers. Though the afternoon was already turning to evening and the shop itself was about to close, there was still a crowd of Saturday shoppers gathered around the counter. Orders were called out loudly to be heard over the din, and hands holding money were held aloft in order to be seen. Annabelle opened the door and found herself in a crowd five deep away.

Though she was taller than most of the people who were snapping up the meat at a voracious pace, she could see no way in which she could ask after Daniel. She tried pushing her way through the crowd gently and politely but quickly found herself shoved backward to her rightful spot in the queue.

"Is Daniel Green here?" Annabelle called, finding her voice drowned out in the loud, rapid slamming of cleaver on chopping board. "I said," she repeated, more loudly, "is Daniel Green here?"

Somehow, one of the assistants who was busily slicing rashers of smoked bacon seemed to hear her.

"Boss!" he called, toward a door at the back. "Boss! Someone here to see you!"

Annabelle turned toward the door and watched a tall, handsome man with a chiseled jawline and crystal-blue eyes emerge. Philippa certainly wasn't overstating the point about him either.

Daniel looked over the crowd and caught Annabelle's eye. She waved at him, and he gestured for her to join him at a space beside the counter.

"Hello," he said, in a pleasant, lilting Cornish burr. "How can I help you?"

"I'm Reverend Annabelle Dixon from St. Mary's church. I'd like to speak with you about something."

Annabelle thought she detected an ever-so-slight cloud of apprehension pass across Daniel's hypnotizingly blue eyes, before dismissing it as the usual mixture of emotion non-church-attendees felt when they first met her. It was a feeling that combined awkwardness at not attending church recently (or ever) with suspicion that she was about to persuade them otherwise in future.

"Um... Of course," Daniel said. "What is it about?"

"Actually, I was rather hoping we could talk somewhere quiet. It's rather important."

"I see," Daniel said, nodding cautiously, a cloud of doubt now blatant upon his face. "Well, I would say we could talk at the pub since it's nearby, but being a vicar I don't—"

"The pub is fine," Annabelle smiled. "Shall I wait for you there?"

Daniel looked surprised but nodded. "Sure. I'll see you there in a few minutes after I've finished up here."

Roughly ten minutes later, Annabelle was sitting at a table near the entrance to the King's Head, sipping gingerly from a half-pint of cider and trying to pace her nibbling of a packet of peanuts so that they lasted as long as possible. Though the King's Head was nowhere near as popular as the Dog And Duck, Barbara's pub, it did very well nonetheless. Especially on Saturdays, when the shoppers who flocked to the nearby market and shops such as Daniel's found it a calming pit stop.

The atmosphere was pleasant. The pub was half-full with families partaking of a hearty meal, regulars indulging in habitual conversations, the subjects of which seemed to comprise only three in number, and working men enjoying the freedom of their weekend. Annabelle gazed at the door absently, until it finally opened and Daniel's tall, athletic frame stepped inside.

"Daniel! Yoo-hoo!" Annabelle called.

Daniel turned his head, and once again, Annabelle felt as if the good-looking man were holding something back. He gestured a brief greeting, before getting the bartender's attention. The barman nodded an acknowledgement as Daniel took a seat opposite Annabelle and settled down.

"I never thought I'd be drinking with a priest in a pub when I got up this morning!" he joked, his laugh slightly guarded.

Annabelle laughed along with him. "I would say the same, but in the life of a church vicar, you learn to expect the unexpected!"

The barman placed Daniel's drink – a pint of dark ale – on the table in front of him and walked away. Daniel grabbed it in his large, strong palm and gulped almost half of it down in one fell swoop.

"Oh, my," Annabelle said. "We've not even said a toast yet."

Daniel laughed nervously, before wiping his lips on the back of his hand.

"Sorry," he stammered.

Annabelle noted the anxious expression of the large man. The working men of Upton St. Mary were a warm, laid-back, talkative bunch, so it was rather alarming to see such a successful tradesman so ill at ease, particularly when in his element. She sipped from her cider slowly, giving her mind time to consider Daniel's bizarre behavior.

Daniel watched her intently, waiting for her to make the first move, to reveal her hand.

"Business certainly seems to be good," Annabelle said.

"Yes," Daniel said, slowly, "it is."

In the silence that followed, the tension between the two grew ever thicker, until Daniel grabbed his pint glass again and finished off his drink in an impressive display. Almost immediately, he turned to the man behind the bar and raised his empty glass. In accordance with the ritual they had obviously practiced over and over, the bartender again nodded back nonchalantly.

"Sorry, Vicar. What exactly is this about?"

Annabelle spun the bag of peanuts around to offer some to the butcher, who refused, shaking his head.

"I wanted to ask you about your upbringing in Upton St. Mary."

"My *upbringing?*" Daniel exclaimed in a voice that sounded extremely relieved, while a look of utter surprise swept across his face.

"Specifically, your girlfriends."

"Ohhhhh!" Daniel smiled, leaning back and nodding. "Lucy? Right?"

"Yes," Annabelle said, taken aback by Daniel's newfound ease.

Daniel chuckled, and for the first time, his humor seemed genuine to Annabelle.

"Well, what do you want to know?"

"Tell me about you and Lucy."

"Okay," Daniel said, receiving his drink from the barman and taking a sip from it that was a lot less ferocious than before. "Let's see. I don't really remember where we met. Everybody knew everyone else back in those days. I asked her out at a dance, and she said yes. We met up the next day, at the church, in fact, and just talked for hours. That was that, really. After that day, we did pretty much everything together. Went to the cinema, took bike rides together. She'd come and watch me play football, I'd go and see her performances."

"Performances? She was an actress?"

Daniel laughed. "She was a little bit of everything! She wanted to be an actress, a dancer, a vet, and a nurse, if you can believe that!"

Annabelle smiled. "How long were you together?"

Daniel screwed his face up in thought. "Under a year, I

think. Not long when you say it like that, but when you're young, it feels like forever."

Annabelle nodded and popped some more peanuts into her mouth. Daniel followed suit, tilting his head back, opening his mouth and dropping them into it.

"Did you love her?" Annabelle asked, as carefully as she could.

Daniel screwed his face up once again, crunching through his peanuts as he searched for the words. His eyes turned pensive as he looked to the side.

"What does a kid know about love at that age?" he said, eventually.

Annabelle shrugged. "You do seem like you were very taken with her."

"I was," Daniel said, his face serious now. "She was a fantastic girl. But Louisa was the one that really took my breath away."

Annabelle almost fell off her chair at this revelation.

"Louisa Montgomery? Her sister? The teacher?"

Daniel nodded, his silence only adding to the conviction behind his words.

"You were in love with Louisa? Not Lucy?"

"Don't get me wrong, Lucy was wonderful. She was pretty, charming, easy to talk to. She was the second most attractive girl in the entire village."

"But Louisa was the first?"

"Louisa was the most beautiful girl I'd ever seen, even to this day," Daniel said, his palm slapping gently on the tabletop as if to emphasize his point. "Pretty girls are ten a penny, but Louisa had something more about her, a quality, a magnetism. She was like a queen. And smart, too. Almost scarily so. I know it's hard to believe looking at her now but she was the kind of girl who made you feel like you were in the presence of something magnificent."

Annabelle found herself stunned into silence at the sincerity and devotion that came through in Daniel's words.

"But..." Annabelle stammered, searching for some logic in this new perspective, "if you felt that way about Louisa and not Lucy, why did you date Lucy and not her sister?"

Daniel leaned back in his chair and opened his palms in a gesture of defeat. "Louisa had a boyfriend. She was taken. Gary Barnes, a boring bloke if you ask me. They were 'childhood sweethearts,' together since they were too young to really know what they were doing. They even got married eventually, but they divorced soon afterward."

"Why?"

"I don't know the details, but Gary worked for a car manufacturer and got offered a position in their American office. He wanted to go, and she didn't. Simple, really. Knowing Gary, though, it makes perfect sense. He was always the kind of person who put work before anything else."

"Hmm," Annabelle said, fishing around in the peanut packet with no luck. Daniel plucked it from the table and waved it in the direction of the bar. The man behind it nodded once more.

"Katie Flynn painted a very different picture of Louisa when I asked about her earlier."

"Bah," Daniel scoffed, "of course she would. She's had it in for her since that whole mess with the tea shop. Katie's always been one to hold a grudge. She's been like that since we were young."

A new packet of peanuts was placed on the table and Daniel opened it for Annabelle as she furrowed her brow in thought.

"Thank you," Annabelle said, plucking a few nuts from the proffered packet and munching on them absent-mindedly.

"Is there a particular reason you're asking about all of this, Reverend?"

Annabelle swallowed and washed the peanuts down with another sip from what little was left of her cider. "Just curiosity," she lied, acceding to the Inspector's wishes for once. "I only recently heard of Lucy's disappearance. It seemed rather odd to me."

"What was odd about it?"

"Well, that she disappeared without a trace. Excuse my directness, but it seemed like, as someone close to her, you would have known what had happened or even been under suspicion yourself."

Daniel laughed nervously. "I was! The police asked me so many questions that I thought I was going to get a grade at the end of it!"

Annabelle's refusal to acknowledge his joke urged Daniel to continue.

"I don't know what happened. I wish I did..."

"When did you last see her?"

"We had gone to the cinema to see a film. A chick flick. Her choice, of course. Afterward, she was in a good mood. We walked about the village and stopped at Benjamin's, a nice pie shop by the library that isn't there anymore. We talked and ate, then I walked her home. Louisa met us at the door, I kissed her goodbye, and that was that."

"When did you realize she was gone?"

"A few days later, we were supposed to meet on the edge of the village, across the woods from Shona Alexander's place. I waited at the bus stop for an hour because she was late. But see, she was always late. I'd get so worked up, but she was the kind of person who could make you forget how angry you were by saying something silly. This time though, I was so cheesed off that I was thinking about how I wouldn't let that happen this time. Eventually, I went home. I called her house, this was before mobile phones, and Louisa told me she was definitely out because she had seen her leave the house. That's when I realized something was up."

"Did anyone see you at the bus stop?"

"Not really. I mean, a few buses went past, but if I asked you who was waiting at a bus stop when you drove past, would you remember?"

"Did anyone else see her leave?"

"Her mother. Her father was dead at that point. Once Louisa told me they had seen her go out the door, I got a bit anxious, still angry, but a little bit worried. I went around the village asking everyone if they'd seen her. Nobody had. That night her mother called the police. The night after that, they were asking me about every conversation we'd ever had. It was like they thought I'd kidnapped her and hidden her somewhere!"

"What do you think happened?"

Daniel thought over the question a little, though it was clear he had an answer ready.

"I think she ran away, to tell you the truth. Like I said, she wanted to be an actress, a singer, have adventures, and see the world. My guess is that she just left, probably to make her fortune in London or some other big city."

"But without telling anyone? Without packing anything?"

Daniel shrugged. "Maybe she was fed up with village life, fed up of the same people. Maybe she wanted a clean break from everything. God knows I've wanted that myself sometimes. Lucy was a poet, an idealist. She probably thought it would be romantic to run away to London one day and see if she could make it with nothing in her pocket. The funny thing is, I'd bet that she could."

Annabelle found Daniel's casual manner in discussing Lucy's disappearance slightly concerning until she reminded herself that he had no idea about the body in the woods. For him, this was a long gone incident that was dead and buried. If he had been aware of the imminent news that the affair was to be revisited, he would almost certainly not have been so open about his dismissive feelings toward Lucy or his still rather strong ones for Louisa.

After sipping the last of her cider, Annabelle placed the glass down softly and looked once again at the attractive face of the man sitting across from her.

"Would you like another?" he asked.

"No, thank you, I should get going."

Daniel looked askance at the Reverend while a playful smile worked its way onto his face.

"Is that really all that you wanted to ask me about, Reverend?"

"Yes, though I may have more to ask you soon. Thank you for your time, Daniel."

Daniel chuckled. "My pleasure. It's always nice to share a pint with someone new."

Annabelle dropped the payment for her drink and peanuts in coins on the table and left Daniel to join some friends of his. As soon as she stepped outside, a cold snap of wind and the surprisingly dark street once again reminded her of the approaching season. She pulled her cassock in around her a little more tightly and began walking.

Annabelle decided not to drive home immediately. After her cider, she needed to wait before she could get safely back behind the wheel. She had an hour to kill so she decided to amble around the village and use the time to think about what she had learned from the surprisingly forthright butcher.

She now had an idea of the time and events that had surrounded Lucy's disappearance, though she was still grappling with wildly differing accounts. The enigmatic Louisa Montgomery was growing ever more difficult to discern. To Katie, she was an introverted shrew who lived in the shadow of her sister's charming personality and radiant popularity. To Daniel, she was a magnetic beauty who surpassed her sister in all aspects, and for whom he would have dismissed Lucy in an instant were Louisa not bound to a dullard since youth.

And still, despite the detailed, honest reports of these two childhood friends who had been present at the time of her disappearance, Annabelle could not ascertain a motive or reason for Lucy's murder, if indeed it was murder.

Feeling the corner of her notepad jut into her waist, Annabelle was reminded once again of her need to deliver the Sunday sermon. She decided to visit the local library. It was always a peaceful, inspiring place for such things, and there, she could focus her thoughts on something other than the mysteries that were causing her such consternation.

With the purpose of a destination in mind, she quickened her pace and took a rather discreet shortcut through a cobblestoned alleyway that always made her feel as if she had stepped back in time to the eighteenth century.

"You can't have her!" came a faint voice from the darkness at the end of the alley. "She's mine! She's always been mine! Who do you think you are to take her from me!?"

Something about the voice seemed familiar to Annabelle, but the anger and aggressiveness threw all of her senses for a spin. Had she stumbled upon a physical altercation? Was somebody in danger? Annabelle flew into a stride that carried her down the short length of the alleyway in seconds, grimly determined to ensure that no harm would come to anybody, her arms raised in preparation for whatever lurked in the shadows.

"She belongs with me! And I'll do everything in my power to keep her!"

As Annabelle drew closer, the silhouette became recognizable. She slowed down as she reached within a few yards of the wildly gesticulating, hurriedly pacing figure who was screaming into his phone.

"Just you try and stop me! She's mine! She's always been mine!"

It was the Inspector, and he was shouting so viciously into his phone that Annabelle could see the spittle flying from his gnarled mouth even in the darkness. She held back, hoping the Inspector would not see her, but when he hung up with an immense amount of frustration, he spun around to walk away and was immediately confronted by the sight of the embarrassed Vicar.

"Ah... Hello Inspector?"

"What do you want? Are you listening in on my conversations now as well?"

"Absolutely not! I was just on my way to the library."

"And you decided to stop and tell me how to do my job again, did you?"

Annabelle's embarrassment was replaced by an assuredness that ran confidently through her in the face of the Inspector's rudeness.

"You were shouting at the top of your lungs, Inspector. You cannot expect privacy when you choose to rant and rave in public so."

The Inspector breathed deeply, unable to find a retort amid the muddled thoughts of his anger.

"Now," continued Annabelle, taking this moment of confusion to assert herself, "I was simply passing when I heard you and if you'd care to calm down and talk reasonably with me, Inspector, I believe I may be able to provide some information that would be pertinent to your current case."

At this the Inspector straightened himself and looked at Annabelle directly.

"Go on."

Annabelle smiled at the Inspector's receptiveness.

"This is terribly exciting, isn't it?" she giggled. "Two people exchanging information in a dark alleyway. It's like a scene from one of those exotic spy films, or a romantic thriller..."

"Reverend..."

"We're almost making a habit of meeting in dark places, Inspector. If I didn't know bett—"

"Please, Reverend. I'm not in the mood. Just tell me what you've found out."

"Yes, of course," Annabelle said, clearing her throat. "Well, I've learned that Lucy's boyfriend at the time of her disappearance was Daniel Green, a local butcher."

"Excellent," the Inspector said sincerely, though his voice still bore the remnants of his earlier fury. "Then we have a suspect."

Annabelle balked at the Inspector's speedy conclusion.

"Oh no! I didn't mean to imply... I mean, perhaps. It's not implausible... But I was by no means saying..."

"What did he tell you?"

"Well, this is the interesting aspect, he told me he wasn't

particularly attached to Lucy at all. In fact, it was *Louisa* that his heart was truly set on."

Even in the darkness Annabelle could see the Inspector's expression settle firmly.

"You've just given me a suspect and a motive, Reverend. This 'butcher' prefers the sister to Lucy, so he offs Lucy and hopes it'll bring him closer to the girl he wants."

"Inspector! Surely you cannot reduce this to something so simple. I am certain there are more layers of complexity to this."

The Inspector sighed deeply, regretting his recent outburst. "You're right. I've just got a lot on my mind. It's a possibility though. We've confirmed the body is Lucy's. She died from a blow to the head, and it appears that she was being regularly beaten throughout her life."

Annabelle gasped. "Surely not!"

"Oh, it's for sure, all right. The forensic anthropologist confirmed it."

"That's dreadful!" Annabelle said.

"These things often are."

Annabelle cast her eyes down mournfully.

"There's something else," Annabelle said, raising her eyes to meet the Inspector's, "I followed Louisa today."

"Is that normal behavior for a Reverend?"

"Is shouting in the street normal for a detective?"

"I'm sorry. Continue."

"Well, she did something rather strange. She visited a shed, over on the allotments at the edge of the village. I waited for half an hour, and she didn't come back out."

The Inspector scratched his stubble as he thought over this.

"Isn't that what people usually do when they're at their allotments?"

"Not really... Perhaps. I found her behavior rather strange. She went there right after her meeting with you. She wasn't dressed for digging. Then she got her groceries. I have a peculiar feeling that there may be something worth investigating in that shed."

The Inspector digested Annabelle's words then shrugged.

"Maybe so, but to check it we'd need a search warrant. And to get a search warrant you need more than a 'peculiar feeling'."

Annabelle brushed off the Inspector's condescension and decided she was far too cold to stay a moment longer. She would much rather go home to a hot cup of tea and a cozy blanket than be outside in the chilly evening air with the crotchety Inspector.

"Well, if I find out anything else I feel is important, I'll let you know, Inspector."

"Hmph."

"Goodbye, Inspector."

Annabelle watched the Inspector march away, stamping his shoes onto the pavement, his shoulders hunched up defensively.

"Hmph, yourself," she muttered, "You're never going to win me over with an attitude like that, Inspector."

CHAPTER SIX

WHEN ANNABELLE ARRIVED back at the church, it was already dark, and the streets had emptied of families, couples, and animated Saturday afternoon shoppers, who had earlier filled the air with chatter. Now the only people who could be seen were the men making their way to the pubs for a few pints, perhaps a game of darts, or a conversation about the day's football results.

Annabelle was so lost among her thoughts that she almost didn't notice the white car that sat in the spot where she usually parked. Annabelle made out the shape of a man slumped over the wheel. She deftly eased her Mini beside the other vehicle and as the lights of her car flashed across him, the man spun around. Annabelle smoothly finished bringing her own car parallel to the other and locked eyes with the rather embarrassed-looking fellow inside it.

The man fidgeted with his keys before placing them in the ignition and starting his engine. He eased off his handbrake, turned his lights on, and then checked his mirrors, only to find the approaching figure of the Reverend in them.

She rapped on his window with her knuckles and leaned down to get a good look at him. He was a decent-looking chap, with wiry curls of neatly cut, brown-grey hair. With his full lips and big, brown eyes that were set beneath thick eyebrows, he had the air of a friendly, undemanding neighbor about him. The kind of man who would never be a hero but always remember a birthday.

When he saw the cheerful and inviting (if somewhat fatigued) smile on the Reverend's face, his embarrassment seemed to disappear. He turned off the engine. Annabelle stepped away from the door, allowing him space to open it. With a deep sigh, he got out of the car.

"Hello!" Annabelle said, with a hint of curiosity in her voice.

"Hello," the man replied, bowing his head slightly.

"I'm Reverend Annabelle, I take it you've come to see me?" Annabelle said, offering her hand.

The man took it and held it limply for a few seconds before pulling away.

"I'm Dr. Robert Brownson. I... Well... I saw the church spire and just... Sorry..."

Annabelle looked back at the church as if to check it was still there. "Yes," she said. "It is rather noticeable, isn't it? No matter where you are in Upton St. Mary, you can see it."

"Yes," Dr. Brownson said. "I saw it from the hills this morning."

"That was you?" Annabelle remarked, pointing toward the hills beyond the cemetery. "I think I saw you make your way to the top of the hill."

Dr. Brownson nodded.

When it was clear he wasn't going to say anything

further, Annabelle said: "Would you like a cup of tea? My cottage is just behind you. I'd appreciate the company."

Dr. Brownson nodded gratefully and followed the Reverend as she led the way to her warm, cozy kitchen.

"So, Dr. Brownson, have you been waiting long?" Annabelle said, as she readied the cups and tea bags.

"Not really. Perhaps. I'm not too sure."

Annabelle frowned at her visitor's confusion. She had had rather an eventful day herself and felt that she had little energy left for yet another mysterious problem. But such is the life of a village priest.

With the teapot full and the cups laid out, Annabelle brought over the plate of shortbread Philippa had left out and took a seat opposite the quiet stranger. The gentle sound of the cat door caught Annabelle's attention before she could speak, and she noticed Biscuit entering the kitchen, her eyes focused on the table.

"Honestly," Annabelle said, "I believe that cat has the ability to detect a sugary treat from the other side of the village."

Dr. Brownson smiled awkwardly as the cat leaped onto his lap and settled herself into a comfortable position.

"May I ask what brings you to this corner of the kingdom, Dr. Brownson?"

"Please, call me Robert," he said, as he tentatively leaned forward over the cat, careful not to disturb her, and measured out half a teaspoon of sugar before dropping it into his cup with great care. "I am a forensic anthropologist. I was called here on business."

Annabelle felt her tiredness evaporate. "The body in the woods?" she blurted out eagerly, before remembering that she had promised the Inspector she would keep it a secret.

"Why yes," Robert said, surprised.

"That's strange," Annabelle said, pursing her lips. "We already have someone who does that kind of thing around here, Dr. Harper Jones."

Robert's expression flickered through a number of emotions before he sighed slowly and abjectly. "Harper is a pathologist."

"Ah yes, of course she is," Annabelle said, emphatically pretending she knew the difference.

They sipped their hot teas, each passing the time by taking a shortbread. Robert slowly stroked the cat in his lap, though Biscuit, seeing that no treats were about to be offered, promptly decided she had had quite enough of their company and leaped down to the floor. In silence, they watched her make her way to the living room where she would no doubt enjoy the luxury of choosing the perfect sleeping spot, the better to be refreshed for her nightly excursion around the village that was just a few hours away. After a minute's silence, Robert's shoulders slumped, and he resolutely placed his teacup down.

"Actually, Harper is the reason that…"

Annabelle waited for an end to the sentence, but the man across the table seemed incapable of concluding any of his thoughts, either in his head or out loud. Annabelle realized that something was troubling him, and that he would need some assistance in discussing it. She placed her own teacup down and leaned forward sympathetically.

"If there is anything troubling you, Robert, you're welcome to talk about it with me, whether it's spiritual or not."

As if realizing how close he was to spilling out his thoughts, Dr. Brownson immediately sat up rigid as a post, an innocuous smile forcefully stretched across his face.

"Ah! It's nothing! A silly notion that will be gone by tomorrow morning."

Annabelle glared at the doctor, unconvinced.

"Hmm. It often takes more than a 'silly notion' to draw people to the spire of the church. People tend only to notice it when they look to the sky for help, having found none elsewhere."

"Really, Reverend..."

"Okay," Annabelle said, shrugging lightly, "I remain unconvinced, however. And if you're unable to convince me that it's not worth talking about, I doubt you'll convince yourself, Robert."

Robert glanced only for a moment at Annabelle, but it was enough to see the sincerity and openness in the Reverend's eyes. He sighed once more and smiled.

"You're sharp, Reverend. I suppose talking couldn't hurt."

"Of course."

Robert nodded, staring at his teacup as he galvanized himself to say things that he had not told anyone.

"It's Harper Jones."

"What about her?" Annabelle said quickly, her tone full of worry.

"Oh, no... Nothing like that," assured Robert when he saw the fear in Annabelle's eyes. "It's just that... she's married."

Robert looked up, deep pain written across his face. Annabelle searched it for some clue as to what exactly the problem was and shook her head when she couldn't find one.

"I'm sorry, Robert. What's the problem?"

Robert sighed again. "I've never been very good at explaining these kinds of things."

"It's fine. Just take a deep breath, and start from the beginning."

Robert did as he was told before speaking again.

"We met just under thirty years ago. I was doing a Ph.D. in biological anthropology at the time. Harper was an undergraduate studying medicine. I remember I had visited the library in search of a specific book, and it wasn't on the shelves. I looked around, and there she was, angelic, yet magnificent. Her skin was almost luminescent, and the determined, penetrating manner in which she read her book was so striking. She had the very book I intended to read."

"Well, over the coming weeks, in the library, this happened again, and again, and again! Sometimes she would seek a certain book that I had already taken from the shelves and had begun to work from. Other times I would arrive at the library and find her using the very one I had come for. We'd exchange knowing nods and patiently wait for the other to finish. Sometimes we would talk, and each time we did we discovered we shared more than a few interests and ideas. It was no coincidence. It was fate!

"We discovered that we had a mutual love of history. We were both enamored with the idea of unlocking the mysteries of things that had once been alive. Our fields were different, but our passions were almost perfectly attuned. We soon began to help each other in our work, Harper's rationality and clarity of thought combining with my rather creative and intuitive approach. Two people with different personalities but the same goals. We were perfectly balanced. There was only one thing we could do..."

"What?" Annabelle interjected, wide-eyed.

Robert looked up with sorrow in his brown eyes.

"Fall in love."

The words hung in the air like the final note of a

symphony, resonating in Annabelle's mind. Dr. Brownson continued, "Of course, Harper caught the attention of most men on campus. She was an extraordinarily beautiful woman. She still is. But Harper has always been a formidable creature of intellect. For us, our love of history and love of ideas easily transformed into a love for each other. We were inseparable for the few years we were together. A more perfectly matched pair you couldn't find! We lived in our very own world of study and simple pleasures. We didn't even argue or disagree as normal couples do. Our only disagreements were academic, and we resolved them using rigorous research and the scientific method. That may sound staid to many, but to two people in love with knowledge, it was the ideal relationship."

"What happened?" Annabelle asked, eventually.

"To put it simply, Reverend, life happened. I have always been an academic at heart. I still am. I love the musty smell of university libraries. The hallowed halls of institutes dedicated to the sole pursuit of pure knowledge. To surround myself with others who are just as focused upon the furthering of science and wisdom as I am is blissful to me. I am, to put it bluntly, a stuffy professor, and always have been. Harper, on the other hand..."

"Likes to get her hands dirty," Annabelle added, helpfully.

"Precisely," nodded Robert, sadly. "She wanted to see the world. To put her knowledge to work in the wild, as it were. She felt that theory was worthless unless one could put it into practice. She was soon gone, regretfully, of course, but gone nonetheless. Her insight and intelligence brought her plenty of attention from other universities around the world and some very inviting prospects, if I say so myself. Eventually she received an offer that was too good to refuse. We stayed in touch for several years, but she was so busy, and I was somewhat... bitter, I'm ashamed to say. I longed for her to return. Indeed, I always expected that she would, but it never happened."

Robert took a bite from his biscuit and then a long sip of his tea, as if concluding his story. However, Annabelle found herself feeling that this was not the end of his tale.

"It's been over twenty years since you last saw her, you say?"

"Yes, twenty-five, in fact."

"And you've not met anyone else in all this time?"

"I know it sounds pathetic, Reverend. Nobody is more aware of that than me. I'm a university professor, however. My kind are not easy with women. There are not many opportunities for me to meet them, and even when I have, it has never worked out. The heart wants what it wants, as they say. After Harper, I found it difficult to compare another woman favorably. No woman could match her, and to delude either myself or them would have been unfair."

"I take it you've spoken to Harper?"

Robert nodded.

"I saw her today. As radiant as ever. I also learned that she was married. It's funny, but now that I know she's gone for good, I feel bereaved. Not just because I finally realize that I've lost her, but because I also feel that I've lost all those years I was waiting for her to return. "

Annabelle reached out her hand and placed it over the doctor's. He smiled appreciatively.

"I know it's stupid of me," Robert continued, "but I almost feel like I should fight for her. I know it's wrong, but to just walk away feels like throwing away nearly thirty years. Years in which not a day passed by when I didn't think about what she might be doing. It has been like walking around with a ghost; one who is there, and yet not there. Always in my peripheral vision, always at the edge of my thoughts."

"I can't say I understand what that is like," Annabelle said, "but there is no 'fight' to be had, Robert. If you don't let Harper go, then you'll never be happy."

"I know, Reverend. But I don't feel as if I'll ever be truly happy without her, either."

Annabelle looked at the pained man in front of her with a deep sense of pity.

"There is joy and happiness waiting for you in the world, Robert. As soon as you open your eyes to it."

"Thank you, Reverend. You know, I was actually supposed to return to London today, but I found myself feeling uplifted by the countryside here, however depressed I've also felt."

"That's good," Annabelle smiled. "Perhaps you've already begun to forge a new beginning for yourself."

"I'd like to think so, Reverend. Though I feel I'm struggling right now."

"These things take time, Robert."

Robert nodded, picked up his teacup and drank the last drops from it. He slowly pulled his hand away from under the Reverend's, returned her smile, and stood up.

"Well, I'm sincerely grateful, Reverend. I know this has been an inconvenience, especially at this late hou—"

"Oh, tosh!" Annabelle interrupted. "It was a pleasure to meet you, Robert. I sincerely hope you find the right path, and I also hope this is not the last time we'll talk to each other."

Robert threw on his coat and made his way to the door.

"I hope so too, Reverend," he gazed at the floor thoughtfully. "You know, I can sort of see why Harper moved to this area. It's beautiful, full of history, and if you're any indication, Reverend, the people are remarkably kind."

Annabelle giggled a little as Robert stepped through the door.

"With charm such as that, Professor, I am sure you won't be wanting of a woman for very long!"

Robert laughed as he waved at the Reverend and got in his car. Annabelle watched his car turn around in the yard and roll through the church gates before closing the door. She walked into the living room, and slumped onto the couch. It seemed that love was very much the theme of the day in Upton St. Mary, though unfortunately only the unrequited and rather destructive kind.

Annabelle had found herself too distracted to formulate the notes and thoughts she usually did when planning a sermon, but the unusual events that had transpired over the previous days along with the many stories she had heard inspired her to give an excellent sermon "off the cuff." In her gentle, humorous, and friendly manner, she delivered a thought-provoking talk about secrets, honesty, and the spiritual benefits of letting go. The quiet, attentive crowd nodded their heads in agreement and smiled their approval as she dispensed advice to her flock.

Annabelle's pleasure at the reception of her spontaneous sermon intensified as she bade goodbye to her congregation at the church doors. They poured praise and compliments on her, some even saying that it was the best they had ever heard. Annabelle accepted their good wishes politely, and when the last church-goer had expressed his gratitude and set off through the gates, she turned back inside with a large smile that seemed to begin from the depths of her heart.

After taking a few steps, however, the positive feelings that seemed to vibrate around her gave way to something more ominous and troubling. Philippa was standing in front of her, her skin once again pale and sickly, stress apparent in her face.

"Reverend..." she uttered reluctantly.

"Yes, Philippa? Is everything alright?"

"Your sermon was very good today, Reverend..."

"Why thank you, Philippa! I'm glad you liked it."

"...It has persuaded me... to think that... I should tell you what's been bothering me, however ashamed I am of it."

Annabelle quickly walked up to her troubled friend and gently brought her toward a pew.

"Of course you should tell me, Philippa. You've no need to feel ashamed when you're with me! After all, we're friends!"

"Thank you, Reverend."

Annabelle sat beside Philippa and patiently waited for her friend to begin.

"Take your time, Philippa."

"Well, it happened about a week ago now... Oh Reverend, I hope you don't think this is terribly un-Godly. I've never had anything like this happen to me before!"

"I won't judge. Just tell me what it is, and we can talk about it."

Philippa took in a deep breath.

"I saw a vision."

"A vision?"

"A terrible vision. Horrifying. I've spent the past week wondering what it might mean. Hoping that it wouldn't happen again."

"I'm sure it's nothing, Philippa. It was probably just a dream, or something just as innocent."

"Oh no, Reverend," Philippa said, looking up at Annabelle with her eyes wide, "this was so vivid. I would swear it was real."

"What was it exactly?"

"It happened during the night, perhaps two or three in the morning. I woke up in order to visit the bathroom. I've been drinking a terribly large amount of tea lately, as I always do when autumn is approaching. I tell you, I always know when the cold weather's about to hit by how many cups I find myself—"

"The vision, Philippa?"

"Oh yes, sorry, Reverend. I suppose my mind isn't keen on remembering it. I was on my way to the bathroom when I heard an awful screaming. Oh Annabelle, it was terrifying. It sounded like the screams of hell, almost animal in its pain. I went to my kitchen window and pulled aside the curtain and...."

Philippa shook her head and buried it in her hands, gasping.

"What was it? What did you see Philippa?"

"It looked like... like a ghost! Running across the field. It was all in white, lit up like the light of the moon."

"A ghost?"

"It was monstrous, Reverend. It was covered in blood, and was wielding some kind of weapon. My body froze, I couldn't move, I wasn't even able to scream. I just went cold all of a sudden, as the figure tore across the field."

"Did you see its face? Perhaps it was a real person?"

Philippa breathed deeply again.

"Its eyes were big and white, and there was a look of fearsome determination. I don't know how, but I could tell this monster was intent upon wreaking destruction. It had the eyes of something evil, something with murderous intent. The eyes, the blood, the shrieking.... I've never seen anything like it. I know it didn't come from my imagination. Even my nightmares aren't as horrible as that!"

Annabelle rubbed Philippa's back gently.

"Perhaps it was something else."

"What else could it be, Reverend? The next day you were even talking about a dead body in the woods!"

"Oh Philippa, I told you that body had been buried for years!"

"Yes, but... perhaps the spirit... or..."

"Come now, don't go letting your imagination run wild. I'm sure there's a perfectly reasonable explanation."

"Like what?"

Annabelle opened her mouth, hoping something logical and rational would pour forth, but she quickly closed it when she found herself out of ideas.

"I... don't know. But that doesn't mean there isn't an explanation."

"I sincerely hope you're right, Reverend," Philippa said, her eyes as pleading and as vulnerable as a child's, "but I'm deeply afraid you're not."

"Would you like a cup of tea?"

"No, thank you. I should get back to tidying the church."

"Indeed. I'll help you."

"No, Reverend. I'd prefer to do it myself. I... like to keep myself occupied. It helps me not to think about it."

Annabelle nodded supportively. "As you wish. If you need anything, just tell me. Try to be patient, I'm sure we'll get to the bottom of this."

"Thank you, Annabelle. I do appreciate it. I hope you don't think I'm going mad."

"Of course not! Why, I've even seen some sights myself lately that I haven't been able to explain."

Philippa grabbed the Reverend's arm tightly and glared at her.

"Such as what, Reverend?"

"Oh, I'm sure it's nothing. And I don't want to feed your already active imagination. I assure you that what I saw was both vivid and bizarre, and has an explanation. I just don't know what it is yet. But I will find out, don't you worry! "

Philippa stood up and began to collect the prayer books from the pews. Annabelle made her way home and considered putting on the kettle, before changing her mind, throwing on her coat, and heading back out to her Mini.

It seemed that Annabelle couldn't take more than a few steps without encountering strange behavior, peculiar incidents, and yet more mysteries. She was used to conundrums, and indeed, she rather enjoyed using her charm and wits to discover the truth behind seemingly odd events. However, she was beginning to feel that the sheer volume of questions she had been trying to answer for days was overwhelming.

First, there was the Inspector's behavior that had become increasingly concerning. He was waspish when she had encountered him in the woods after Dougie tripped over the bone, behavior that Constable Raven had told her had been a consistent theme for weeks. Following the incident with Terry's dog, Annabelle knew that the Inspector was not only growing increasingly erratic and temperamental, but also that he would be fairly ineffectual in getting to the bottom of the very case he was in Upton St. Mary to pursue. His shouted phone call in the alleyway still resonated in her mind. Was he involved in some kind of love triangle? As far as Annabelle knew, the Inspector had divorced years ago and had been single for a while now. However, the romantic overtones of his cryptic demands were unavoidable. As she frowned at the memory of the shouted phone call, Annabelle found herself feeling a little envious of whoever had managed to place such a stranglehold on the Inspector's affections but quickly swept the feeling away before it took too firm a hold.

Now there was Philippa's "vision." Though she was deeply religious, Annabelle could not entertain any notion of it being a spiritual one, knowing only too well that Philippa had an imagination that ran as wild and free as the wind. But her friend had obviously seen something that had initiated such horror in her mind, although even Annabelle's easy ability to jump to far-reaching conclusions failed her when she tried to explain it.

Finally, there was the increasingly complex matter of Lucy's death. The body in the woods had been confirmed as Louisa's sister, and the Inspector had revealed that she was murdered, but in her quest to discover a possible killer, or even a motive, she had been met only with contradictions and misunderstandings.

She could not shake the idea that Daniel Green's behavior at the beginning of their meeting was highly suspicious, and the way he had loosened up when talking about Louisa perturbed her. As the most plausible suspect, it was the opposite of what she had expected. Likewise, Louisa's mysterious and oddly-timed trip to a shed on the allotments had seemed very peculiar to Annabelle, though the

Inspector was correct in saying that it indicated nothing very much of anything at all.

Most confusing had been the difference in the stories she had heard from Katie Flynn and Daniel Green. Katie's had no doubt been colored by her conflict with Louisa. It also wasn't clear that she was a reliable witness. Daniel's story had seemed almost too extraordinary to be believable. Had he constructed his story about having feelings for Louisa to suit some ulterior motive? If so, why?

Annabelle knew she had to get the story from an unbiased source. A person who had been around at the time, but who had not been involved. A person who was tuned in to all of Upton St. Mary's gossip, past and present. Someone who was guardian of the village's secrets, who saw people at their worst, but also at their best.

Annabelle parked her beloved Mini outside The Dog and Duck and stepped out of it. It was time she talked to Barbara Simpson, the pub landlady, once again.

"Reverend!" she called, as she watched Annabelle enter. "Have you come for that lunch I promised? Wouldn't be surprised if you'd worked up an appetite, I heard your sermon was a good one today."

Annabelle smiled as she stepped toward the bar, behind which Barbara was sporting a leopard-print blouse and hoop earrings so large they could have been frisbees. Her long eyelashes fluttered with glee, and she seemed to radiate a warm, inviting aura that encouraged the good-natured laughing of the Sunday drinkers as she chatted back and forth with them.

"Actually," Annabelle said, "I was rather hoping you would have time for a chat."

"Oh," Barbara said, as if greatly honored by the attention, "well, in that case, we should have a drink. What'll you have?"

Barbara was already fixing herself a white wine when Annabelle responded.

"Just an orange juice would be fine."

"Orange juice, it is. Let's go over here," Barbara said, as she sidled around the bar and carried the drinks to the booth in the corner.

"So what is it, Vicar?" Barbara said, after sipping heartily from her wine.

"Well it's—"

"Don't tell me, it's Lucy. That was her body in the woods, wasn't it?"

Annabelle considered the right response for a moment, but hesitation was all Barbara needed. She had a lifetime of experience reading faces.

"I knew it! Don't worry, Vicar, I won't tell anybody. Though there are a few people who've already made the connection. "

"Hmm, well I suppose it's a fairly obvious one."

Barbara shook her head sorrowfully.

"Such a sad story."

Annabelle leaned forward.

"What is the story, exactly? I've heard so many versions of the tale, but I still don't feel like I truly know what happened all those years ago between Lucy, Louisa, and Daniel."

"Ah yes," Barbara smiled, her blue eye shadow seeming to brighten as she recalled the memory. "The 'love triangle.' It went on for ages."

"What do you mean?"

"Well, you have to go back very far to get the full story, Vicar. You see, they all grew up together. Louisa, Lucy,

Daniel, and all the rest. They were all born within a few years of each other, and they were like a pack of wolves, I tell you! No, they were nice kids, really. Anyway, Louisa and Gary were both very quiet, intense kids. Both liked to read, both liked to be indoors. You could tell they would become a couple even before they knew it. Well, the thing was, Louisa grew up a real knockout. Oh, you should have seen her! Maybe one of the most beautiful girls I've ever seen in Upton St. Mary. She could have been a film star! Everybody said she was destined for great things. You know when you can just see it in someone? She was smart, too. She was still quiet, but she could have a laugh. Still loved being indoors, but you'd see her at a dance every once in a while usually surrounded by boys. Oh, the boys loved her, for sure."

"Including Daniel?"

"Especially Daniel! He ruled the roost! He was always a mischievous one, that Daniel. He was a bit older than her, but if any of the boys were going to have a chance, and in my opinion she was out of all their leagues, it was Daniel. The only problem was that she was still with Gary. He was a nice enough chap, don't get me wrong, but let's just say she made her choice before she even knew she had one."

"So Daniel began courting Lucy, instead?"

"Right. Lucy was a gorgeous girl too, but next to Louisa... Well, even Marilyn Monroe would have competition."

"Did Lucy and Louisa get along well?"

Barbara pursed her lips a little.

"Not really. It was a little strange, to be honest. Get either of them alone, and they were fine, but put them in the same room, and it was almost as if Lucy lost a little of her shine, and Louisa got a little more bossy. I think there was always a little jealousy between them. Lucy didn't like it that Louisa was prettier and bossed her around. Louisa didn't like it that Lucy was outgoing and loved by everyone for her personality and charm. I heard that they fought constantly behind closed doors."

"Hmm," Annabelle murmured. "That's certainly similar to what I heard."

"Oh, but that's not even half of it, Vicar," Barbara said eagerly, touching the Reverend's arm to add emphasis. "It gets much more complicated."

"How so?"

"Louisa fell in love with Daniel!"

"What?!"

Barbara nodded.

"She never said it, not to any of us, anyway, but it was obvious. You could tell by the way she looked at him, by the way she acted. You see, when Daniel began courting Lucy, he was suddenly always around Louisa too. Going to her house, asking Louisa where her sister was, having Louisa as their chaperone. Daniel was a handsome lad himself, and charming, too. It turns out all he needed was some time to work his magic. It was patently obvious that they both liked each other. Suddenly it wasn't just Gary who was Daniel's problem, it was Lucy too. Louisa started bossing her around even more, stopping her from going out with Daniel, asking her all these questions."

"There's one thing I just can't understand though, if all you're saying is true."

"No word of a lie, Vicar!"

"But in so many years, since Louisa's divorce and Daniel being single still, why have they never gotten together?"

Barbara shrugged.

"Beauty fades, Vicar, as does love. Plus, when Lucy disappeared, it affected everyone badly, especially their friends. They were never the same. No more regular Friday night dances, no more gatherings in the market square, no more parading through the streets like a marching band on its day off. Their group of friends broke up. Sure, they were still around, but they grew up the very night that Lucy disappeared."

"It's a tragic story."

"That it is, Vicar. Louisa got married to Gary as soon as she turned eighteen, went to university, and came back to teach. She barely spoke a word to anyone about anything, let alone about the past. Nobody even knew she was getting divorced until Gary came in one night with his bags packed saying he was going to America. Daniel got himself an apprenticeship, despite being a lazy so-and-so, and worked his socks off every day. Lucy had been like a free spirit in the town. When she disappeared, it was like she took all the childhoods of the village with her. Even I ended up taking a job at the florist's so that I'd have something to do during the summer. The dances and the company just weren't the same when she went. It was such a shame, Vicar."

"Thank you, Barbara," Annabelle said, gratefully, "I can't tell you how much of a help you've been."

"I don't know why you're asking about all of this, Vicar," Barbara said, downing the last of her wine, "and for once, I'd rather not know. Some things belong to the past and are better left to rest there."

CHAPTER SEVEN

ANNABELLE LEFT THE pub with her head
spinning. So much so that she failed to notice the
sight of Dr. Brownson carrying what looked like
paint, an easel, and palette into the pub. He nodded
warmly, but Annabelle decided not to stop and chat. She
had far too much to think about, and a distraction was the
last thing she needed.

Once again, her impression of what had gone on
between Louisa, Daniel, and Lucy all those years ago had
been completely turned around. Now she had a complex
tale of fate, unrequited love, passion, and jealousy to chew
over as she got inside her Mini.

Annabelle paused before starting her engine. Despite
the huge amount of information she had gathered, there was
still simply not enough for her to come to a conclusion. The
more she learned, however, the more enigmatic Louisa
became, and thus the more Annabelle wondered what
Louisa kept in her allotment shed. It was, of course, entirely
likely that there was nothing of any consequence in there,

that Louisa had merely gone to the shed to gain some respite from the village she seemed to find so tiresome. Many a man would understand her sentiment entirely! But Annabelle felt that she had seen something in the manner of the teacher as she made her way toward the allotment. A strange atmosphere of grim determination and loss. A hurrying gait. Signs of a person who has an important thing to do or see.

She brought the key up to the ignition but hesitated once again.

The Inspector was right. There could be an entirely rational explanation. The shed could be filled with nothing but gardening tools and bags of seeds. Annabelle thought of herself as very much a rational person, but her instincts were inflamed with curiosity concerning the shed. Barbara's story had only made her more intrigued by the teacher and her erratic behavior, and Annabelle felt there had to be some side of her that she had not yet seen. Some secret that would not be revealed lightly.

She turned the key and fired up the engine with an air of purpose. The engine roared into life as if agreeing with her decision. She would find Inspector Nicholls, and they would discover the shed's secret, even if there weren't one.

As she puttered slowly toward the Upton St. Mary police station, she caught sight of Constable Jim Raven walking in the opposite direction. She gave a cheery beep to grab his attention and slid the car into a nearby parking spot.

"Hello, Reverend. Heard you had a successful sermon today," the officer said as she exited the car.

"Oh, thank you, though I doubt it will persuade you to attend in future."

Constable Raven laughed to hide his embarrassment.

"Well, I'm so busy... And I do like my Sundays..."

Annabelle waved away the Constable's weak excuses as she drew close.

"I'm looking for Inspector Nicholls. Is he in the station?"

Constable Raven sighed as if exhausted at the mere mention of the Inspector's name.

"Yes, he is, which is why I'm outside. He's getting worse, if anything."

"You mean his temper?"

The Constable nodded. "I still have no idea why."

"I think I might," Annabelle said.

Constable Raven's eyes almost doubled in size as he leaned forward.

"Well, tell me!" he pleaded.

Annabelle shrugged a little to indicate her lack of confidence in what she was about to say.

"I heard him shouting down his phone. About a woman, I think. I can't be sure."

"What did he say?" asked the Constable, with none of the methodical detachment one would expect from a police officer.

"'I want her back.' 'She's mine.' 'You can't take her from me.' Various things to that effect."

Raven folded his arms and looked to the side with a furrowed brow as he digested this information.

"That's rather strange. The Inspector spends all his time either sleeping or at work. He barely meets any women. Hmm, let me think. There's the female officers at

Truro, of course, but all of those are either taken or much too young... The girl in the canteen... but she's covered in tattoos and piercings. Not his thing at all. He practically recoils when she hands him a plate of her Chicken Alfredo. There's the office cleaning lady but she's sixty if she's a day... They're all the women I can think of. And Harper Jones, of course."

Suddenly it was Annabelle who leaned in with keen interest.

"Harper Jones?"

Constable Raven stared confusedly at the Reverend for a few moments before laughing off the idea.

"Give over! Harper Jones isn't that kind of woman. Plus she's married!"

"I wasn't insinuating anything!" declared Annabelle.

"Though Dr. Jones is a bit of a closed book. I mean, what do we know about her really? Have you ever met her husband?"

Annabelle found herself too deep in thought to speak, prompting the Constable to ask, "Reverend? You alright?"

"Oh, yes. I was just thinking. The Inspector wouldn't be the first man I'd met recently who was fighting for the attention of Dr. Jones. Perhaps there is something to it..."

Constable Raven chuckled away the thought.

"I think we're trying to explain the unexplainable, Reverend. Better not to know than to have the wrong idea. We'll just have to wait for it to pass, I suppose."

"Yes, I suppose."

"Well, see you around, Reverend."

"Bye, Constable."

Annabelle hurriedly made her way into the police station, and after exchanging pleasantries with the desk sergeant, she was shown into the office the Inspector had adopted as his own since the investigation in Upton St. Mary had begun.

True to recent form, the Inspector was slumped over, head in hands. She saw he was immersed in the examination of various documents that were frayed and brown from years of being stuffed in gloomy cabinets, no doubt cases that had been filed around the time of Lucy's disappearance.

She knocked gently on the door and waited for the Inspector to raise his head and notice her. It took one more knock, but eventually he huffed, looked at the Reverend, rolled his eyes, and then leaned back in his chair.

"What is it?" he asked curtly.

"I see you're still entrenched in your bad mood as firmly as you are in this case, Inspector."

Nicholls sighed deeply, and Annabelle took the Inspector's lack of words as an invitation to sit across the desk from him.

"Not for long," the Inspector growled as he tossed aside the document and pulled another from the tall pile beside him. "If I don't find anything substantial today, I'm going to close this case. I've got more important things to attend to back in Truro."

"You can't be serious!?" Annabelle burst. "This is a murder!"

"Nearly twenty years old. The trail is too cold at this point to make meaningful progress, let alone solve the case, close it, and secure a conviction."

"What on earth do you mean?"

Again, DI Nicholls sighed deeply, as if too tired to expend the effort of explaining himself.

"Look, Reverend. A young, pretty girl found dead in the woods is the kind of case that you'll find up and down the country, across the world, I daresay. It only takes one passing madman, the wrong kind of meeting with a lunatic in a quiet area. It's not nice, and it's not something you come across frequently out here among your tea shops and village fêtes, but it happens. There's nothing here. If there were, we'd have found it by now."

Annabelle knit her brow, gravely disappointed with the Inspector, and pushed aside the recent idea that he may not be as pure of heart as she had thought. She couldn't fully convince herself that the Inspector was indulging in such devilish behavior as chasing a married woman like Harper Jones. However, confronted with the brutal dismissiveness of his current thinking, she found herself wondering more and more.

"Before you drop this case, Inspector, I must make a strong request."

A raised eyebrow was Nicholls' only response.

"The allotment shed," Annabelle said, raising her hand to stop the Inspector speaking when he immediately began shaking his head. "I have found out rather a lot in the past couple of days regarding Lucy's life at the time of her disappearance, and I believe that whoever is responsible for this terrible deed may be closer than your 'random lunatic'."

"Okay, Reverend," the Inspector said after a moment's thought. "You have two minutes to persuade me."

Annabelle breathed deeply, placed her hands on the table, and began eagerly. She told the Inspector everything, from the unfulfilled desire Louisa and Daniel had had for one another, to the acrimonious relationship between Lucy and her sister. She even told him of the strange behavior Daniel had exhibited when she had spoken to him, and the rush with which Louisa had made her way to her allotment. Her story took far longer than two minutes, but the Inspector listened intently, possibly due to the fact he and his police team had uncovered very little of what Annabelle had managed to on her own. She spoke sincerely and passionately, putting all her charm and persuasiveness to work in order to get through the Inspector's tough shell.

"...if there is a secret yet to be discovered, a clue, then it has to lie with Louisa, and thus, the best chance we have of finding it is in that shed," Annabelle concluded, her eyes fixed upon the Inspector as she waited for his reaction.

He scratched his head for half a minute, sighed, and looked around his desk at the mess of paperwork he had sifted through, as he considered all of the Reverend's points.

"Okay," he muttered, eventually. "This case is a dead end anyway. But if there's nothing in the shed, Reverend, don't expect me to take your opinion seriously ever again. You're putting my trust in you on the line, here."

Annabelle nodded, her lips closed tightly for fear of changing the Inspector's mind once again.

Nicholls stood up, and walked to the door of his office.

"Where's Raven?" he shouted.

"He's just gone out," called Constable Colback, a slight tremor in his voice.

"The lazy so-and-so... You'll have to do the paperwork yourself then, Colback."

Colback mumbled for a few moments before managing to articulate himself more clearly.

"What paperwork's that, Chief?"

Nicholls emitted a sigh that was almost belligerent this time. "The search warrant on Louisa Montgomery's allotment! Do keep up, Colback!"

After increasingly exasperated calls from the Inspector, Colback had pulled in every favor with the Truro station he could to have the Inspector's search warrant ready in double-quick time. When it was ready, Detective Inspector Nicholls snatched it out of the young officer's hand with a glare and set off for his car. With Annabelle in the passenger's seat offering him directions to the allotment, the Inspector drove with the same quick temper and aggression that he had maintained since he arrived in the village. It was an experience that Annabelle, who prided herself on her exceptional driving skills and her respect for the speed limit, found deeply disturbing.

"Who examined the body, by the way?" Annabelle asked innocently after they'd arrived at their destination and she'd caught her breath.

"Harper," grunted the Inspector, "and some big shot from London."

Annabelle nodded.

"Harper's rather nice, isn't she?"

"She's a professional. Doesn't mess around. That's what I like," answered the Inspector, shooting her a glance.

"She's married, is she not?"

At this, the Inspector growled roughly. "Why would I care?" Then, under his breath, "Marriage is for fools. Pointless piece of paper that no one should pay any attention to."

Try as she might, Annabelle couldn't hide the concerned frown that emerged on her face. Suddenly all manner of dots connected up in her mind. Could the Inspector really be involved in a love triangle? With Harper and her husband!

They reached the allotments and got out of the car, the

Inspector slamming his door so hard that Annabelle shrieked a little at the sound. Carefully avoiding the nettles that had so pained her during her previous visit, she and the Inspector traipsed up the path that she had watched Louisa walk days earlier.

"It's just over here, Inspector."

"Hmph."

"Oh dear," Annabelle said, as she reached the shed door. "I completely forgot that the shed was locked when she—"

She turned around to address the Inspector just in time to see him retrieve a menacing-looking crowbar from his long coat and snap the locks apart as if they were made of flimsy plastic.

"Good thinking, Inspector."

"Police procedure, Reverend."

They exchanged a look to confirm their preparedness for whatever lay behind the shed door before DI Nicholls reached out and opened it carefully, peering into the gap as if something might leap out and attack him. When he had opened it enough to be sure nothing dangerous lay inside, he yanked the door open fully. Annabelle quickly followed him inside.

Nicholls cast his eyes over the sacks of soil, the dusty tools that lay haphazardly on the table, and the extensive range of other equipment piled up along the shed's walls. Dust motes floated in the slivers of light that pierced the gloom, the air filled with an aroma that could only be called "eau de gardening."

"Looks like we hit the jackpot," he muttered, in a tone unmistakably sarcastic.

"We certainly might have," Annabelle responded, as she brushed past the Inspector to the far end of the shed.

After pulling aside some brooms and a worn-looking stool, she looked over her shoulder at the Inspector.

"It's a cabinet?" he asked, frowning. "So what?"

Annabelle found the handles, and in a slow, steady gesture, pulled open the doors.

"Gosh!"

"Jesus Christ!"

Hanging in front of them, inside the cabinet among the dirty, old tools and gardening paraphernalia, was an elegant and striking wedding dress. The delicate white fabric seemed to glow in the murkiness and the intricate embroidery made everything in the shed seem even older and dirtier than it was.

They were both shocked to find this alien object in the most unlikely of places but the Inspector was the first one to come to his senses. He stepped toward the cabinet and pulled at a large suitcase which rested at its foot. After fiddling with the clasps he yanked it open.

"This is ever so strange," Annabelle muttered, as the Inspector foraged among clothes and toiletries that were obviously rather dated.

Something drew Annabelle's eye to the side of the cabinet. She carefully reached in to pull it out. It was a shoebox, but when she picked it up the weight seemed rather light for a pair of shoes. The Inspector stood beside her as she slowly lifted the lid. It was packed with yellowed tissue paper and she rustled around to pick out what was packed inside.

"Jewelry," muttered the Inspector.

"Wedding bands, and a necklace to be precise," replied Annabelle.

"Junk, to be even more precise," the Inspector retorted, "but incriminating junk, nonetheless."

Annabelle frowned as she dropped the solitaire diamond necklace back into the box.

"Inspector! Please don't allow your personal issues to cloud this!"

The Inspector looked back at Annabelle with almost angry disdain.

"My personal issues? What do you know of my personal issues!?"

"I know that they've become incredibly disruptive! As does anyone who has had the displeasure of being in your presence recently!"

The Inspector's hands went to his hips and he glowered at the Reverend.

"My personal issues are just that, Reverend – personal! Don't mistake me for a member of your flock, Vicar. I'm not looking for advice or guidance."

"Well, I should think not, Inspector," Annabelle said haughtily, taking a stance just as adamant. "You shouldn't need me to tell you that what you are doing is wrong!"

The Inspector's face seemed to redden even further.

"Wrong? How can... Who are... I am... I am not wrong! She belongs with me!"

"Harper is married, Inspector! She belongs with her husband!"

"What are y—"

"To think a grown man of your age, an Inspector in the police force, no less, would be chasing a married woman in such an impertinent, insolent manner is frankly shameful, Inspector!"

"Rever—"

"And it's no surprise to me, that regarding the circumstances of this case, you are struggling to see reason. You are acting quite disgracefully!"

"Are you quite finished, Reverend?"

Annabelle raised her chin and snorted dismissively.

"Let me put you clearly in the picture, Vicar. You have got the wrong end of the proverbial stick. I am not, as you so enthusiastically put it, 'chasing a married woman.' Least of all, Harper."

"The evidence—"

"The 'evidence'," interrupted the Inspector, crossly, "that you have gathered is clearly faulty, because the only 'female' I've been fighting over recently is a prize bitch."

Annabelle dropped the box of jewelry and gasped in horror. Her hand flew to her mouth.

"My Labrador by the name of 'Lulu,' to be precise. A former Crufts winner I took ownership of thirteen years ago and who has been my best friend ever since. My ex-wife is currently claiming that the dog belongs to her and has reopened our divorce settlement, despite it being two years old. She wants to gain custody of her."

Annabelle dropped her hand and began blushing so furiously that the Inspector wondered if her cheeks would explode. She looked at the ground and placed her hands on her hot face as if to cool it.

"I'm terribly sorry, Inspector. I heard you on the phone and I thought... I... I've made an utter and complete fool of myself."

"Hmph," the Inspector stared at her, his arms folded across his chest.

They stood there for a moment in the dark, the wedding dress hanging behind them, the jewelry at their feet, before the Inspector sighed dejectedly.

"It's okay. So long as you don't mention it outside this shed, I won't either. You're allowed a mistake after finding this," he said, gesturing to the uncommon haul they'd discovered in the shed.

Annabelle nodded shamefacedly, brushing her cheeks to soothe her embarrassment. She was mortified.

"What is this?!" came a shrieking voice from beyond the shed door.

Annabelle and the Inspector spun around to see the beige figure of Louisa, her carpet bag dropped to the ground, clutching her face in horror.

"We had reason to believe that you were hiding evidence, Miss Montgomery," said the Inspector, stepping toward her with the search warrant in hand. "Do you mind explaining what all this is?"

"This," Louisa spat, her voice filled with spiteful anger, "is Lucy's. I've been keeping it since she disappeared, and you have no right to go through it!"

She pushed past the Inspector into the shed and began rearranging the items within the suitcase. Annabelle glanced from Louisa, to the wedding dress, then back to the Inspector, who raised his eyebrows and gestured for the Reverend to join him outside, leaving the appalled teacher in peace.

When they had walked a few steps away, out of earshot, Annabelle clasped the Inspector's arm.

"What do you make of this, Inspector?"

"Well, Lucy was obviously ready for a wedding, and a quick one too, judging by the suitcase. Now, that leaves me with two lines of inquiry. Either she was planning to get married to Daniel or somebody else. Either way, he should have known something about it. The fact that he didn't mention anything about that to you is a pretty clear indicator that he's hiding something."

"Hiding what?"

"My guess is that he's the murderer," the Inspector said, marching off toward the car. Annabelle took one last look at the forlorn figure of Louisa, delicately rearranging the jewelry in the shoebox under the ominous gaze of that magnificent wedding dress, and turned around to run after him.

CHAPTER EIGHT

O
NCE AGAIN, ANNABELLE clung to the passenger-side door handle and hummed her disapproval at the speed and level of aggression with which the Inspector drove. He was even more erratic than before as he zoomed through the narrow streets of Upton St. Mary toward the police station.

"Inspector, are you sure this isn't incredibly rash?" Annabelle managed to blurt out in between the sound of screeching tires.

"We'll give him a chance to explain himself," the Inspector replied, "but he's going to need a hell of a good story to get out of these knots."

Annabelle almost screamed as the Inspector brought the car to a stop inches away from Annabelle's Mini, so sure was she that he would drive straight into it. He leaped out and sprinted up the steps and through the entrance of the station.

"Raven! Colback! Get another car, we're going to arrest Daniel Green."

"The butcher, sir?" Raven asked, confusedly.

"Yes."

Raven and Colback exchanged brief looks before slapping on their hats and running outside.

Annabelle was standing on the pavement as the three officers jumped into their vehicles. Suddenly, sirens were blaring and flashing blue lights were blinding her. Before she could call out to one of the officers, the two cars – one containing Raven and Colback, the other the Inspector – had swarmed into the street and off into the distance. She hurried over to her Mini, miffed at the ease with which the police officers had left her behind and drove off to follow them.

Though she felt very much a part of this operation and was caught up in the noisy thrill and excitement of the racing police cars, Annabelle refused to break the speed limit. She quickly found herself left far behind. By the time she reached Daniel Green's butcher shop, he was already exiting it, accompanied by the constables on either side.

The Inspector followed closely behind. A small crowd of shoppers and Daniel's colleagues gathered at the door of the shop to observe the unexpected turn of events. Nobody, however, seemed more taken aback than Daniel, who had obviously been hard at work when the officers had found him. He was wearing his full butcher's garb, bloodied and messy, and was staring about him at the flashing lights and officious constables as if struggling to make sense of it all.

Annabelle watched from behind the wheel as they put Daniel into the back of the Inspector's car and swerved briskly away again, back toward the police station. Bystanders quickly turned to one another to chatter and speculate on what it was all about as they watched the police cars race into the distance as quickly as they had arrived.

Seeing Daniel had given Annabelle an idea, though she wasn't quite sure what it was. Her instincts told her that there was something terribly wrong with the arrest. Without having the time she needed to formulate her thoughts, she spun the Mini around and once again began her pursuit of the police vehicles returning to the station.

As she drove along, again minding the speed limit, her thoughts raced much faster than her car. The sight of the butcher in his blood-spattered butcher's clothing was stirring some memory at the back of her mind, but what was it? She couldn't quite catch it.

She reached the police station and locked her car carefully before running inside. Just as she was about to rush past the desk through to the back where the interview rooms and offices were, Constable Colback stepped in front of her.

"I'm sorry, Reverend. The Inspector is about to interview someone, I'm afraid you'll have to—"

"Let her through, Colback!" came the Inspector's distinctive, irritated voice from the back. "Lord knows I'd rather have her with me in the interview room than you!"

Annabelle shot the Constable an apologetic look, but he was too embarrassed to catch her eye and simply slunk off to the side. She stepped toward the hallway that led off in the direction of the interview rooms, where the Inspector was waiting impatiently.

"He's waiting for us," the Inspector said, triumphantly, "all we have to do now is get the confession. Shouldn't be too hard considering how much we know."

"I'm not too sure that—"

"Come on, Reverend," the Inspector said, briskly, as he opened the door and gestured her inside.

"You!" Daniel said, as he saw the Vicar enter, followed by the Inspector.

Annabelle met his eyes and nodded a somewhat indecisive greeting. Daniel was sitting behind a table, his hands and clothes still bloody. At this close distance Annabelle could smell the freshly cut beef, pork and lamb emanating from him.

"What's... What's all this about?" Daniel pleaded, his eyes darting between the two visitors.

The Inspector glared silently at him as he pulled out a chair for Annabelle and then sat down himself. Daniel's eyes bore the look of being found out that the Inspector knew only too well, his tense body language demonstrating signs that he was hiding something. The Inspector was suddenly very sure he had made the right choice.

"This is about the truth, Daniel Green. The truth behind what happened that day in the woods between you and Lucy."

Daniel mouthed some words incomprehensibly, and his face turned from expression of fear into one of sheer incredulity.

"What?"

"Lucy's murder. Your ex-girlfriend."

"That was twenty years ago!"

"Justice doesn't come with an expiration date."

"This is crazy!"

"Why didn't you tell us that you were planning to marry Lucy?" the Inspector said, calmly.

Daniel shook his head in a gesture of utter befuddlement.

"Marriage? I was nineteen! I never intended to marry her!" Daniel looked down at his hands, still shaking his head at the absurdity.

"Well, she seemed to be very much of the impression somebody was about to marry her. She was about to turn sixteen. Had herself a nice little wedding dress and a suitcase already packed."

Daniel looked up at the Inspector.

"I don't understand."

"We just found them, over on the allotments. Her sister's been keeping them all this time."

"What... That... That doesn't make sense..."

The Inspector looked at Annabelle, but her face was fixed upon Daniel's in a look of pity. He waited for Daniel to add something meaningful to his confused mumblings, but the butcher only clasped his hands and glanced around him looking deeply perplexed.

"Okay. Let's say for a second that you weren't planning to marry Lucy. Who else could have been?"

Daniel shook his head once again, breathing deeply under the weight of the question's implications.

"It doesn't make sense."

"You said that already."

"No, Detective. I mean, it really doesn't. You see, Lucy wasn't the marrying type at all. She had so many things that she wanted to do. To be a singer, an actress. To travel the world. To meet new people. She never wanted to be tied down. She joked about marriage sometimes, but I think really she just thought it was very boring. She wanted to be young and free forever."

The Inspector sighed deeply.

"Maybe you didn't know her as well as you think you did."

Daniel hung his head.

"I don't know anything anymore. I don't know what to tell you, Detective."

Suddenly, the Inspector slammed his palm upon the table loudly.

"Enough! We've got all the evidence we need to put you away, Daniel Green! This act won't get you anything but a longer sentence! If you've got half as much brains in your head as you've got smeared over your apron there, then you'll talk!"

"But I don't know anything! I don't know how she died!"

The Inspector leaped from his seat and grabbed at Daniel's bloodied butcher's clothes from across the table, pulling the man's face up to his.

"You butchered her just like you butchered one of your animals! This time, though, it's me who will be eating you for breakfast!"

"Inspector!" shouted Annabelle, as she stood up and pulled his arms away from Daniel. "Please!"

The Inspector looked at her for a moment and then, like he were an uncooperative child, Annabelle gently but firmly ushered him out of the interview room, though he kept his stern glare fixed upon the frightened butcher all the way. She pushed the detective outside with a gentle shove and closed the door, leaving Daniel alone in the room behind them.

"This guy knows we don't have much to go on," said the Inspector, pacing up and down while rubbing his brow in frustration, "but he's hiding something. Of that I'm sure."

"Perhaps, Inspector, but you'll not get anywhere if you frighten him half to death!"

"I don't see how else we're ever going to put this case to bed."

Annabelle sighed as she watched the Inspector pace himself into a modicum of calmness. Suddenly a thought flashed across her mind like a bolt of lightning. She realized that the peculiarly familiar feeling she had had when seeing Daniel emerge from the butcher's shop mid-arrest could provide the answer to another question that had been plaguing her for a while. She clicked her fingers, and with a tone of sudden enthusiasm said:

"I have a strong suspicion that I know what our butcher may be hiding."

The Inspector stopped dead in his tracks and looked at Annabelle.

"But it may not actually help us in this case," she added.

"Right now I don't think anything will. But if it explains that man's behavior in any way, then it's worth a shot."

Annabelle nodded as she reopened the door to the interview room.

"Daniel," she said, calmly, as she sat opposite him. The Inspector decided to stand in the corner, hands in pockets, and subject Daniel to nothing but his focused glare. "Did you do anything.... um, peculiar, one night about a week ago?"

The change in Daniel's expression was impossible not to notice. His teeth clenched and his eyes fixed unblinkingly on the Reverend's face.

"I... Don't know... No. I didn't."

"You weren't outside? After midnight?"

"No... I..." he gulped, "What night was this? I'm sorry. I would have to check."

Annabelle looked over toward the Inspector, who was now wearing a look of intense anticipation, not unlike the one Biscuit wore when she was about to pounce.

"I think you may remember this. You were over by Hughes House, where Philippa lives. I believe you know her."

Daniel's eyes widened, and the shortness of his breath was visible in the rapid rising and falling of his chest.

"You were wearing your butcher's clothes," Annabelle continued, "and they were as bloodied and messy as they are now. Philippa saw you."

Daniel slumped over in defeat, before raising his eyes to greet Annabelle's.

"You know, don't you, Reverend?"

Annabelle remained silent.

Daniel shook his head, and with a deep intake of breath, began talking.

"It was an accident. A stupid one, but an accident nonetheless."

"What was?" came the Inspector's gruff tone from the corner of the room.

"I was slaughtering a couple of pigs over on Hughes' farm. I do it a couple of times a week on the quiet, see, and I've done it hundreds of times," Daniel said, as if excusing himself, "but that night I got a little... distracted."

"By what?"

Daniel shuffled in his seat, awkwardly.

"I'd had a few beers. Maybe a few too many," he said, before loudly exclaiming: "It was the night of the England game! We'd played so well! I mean, you'd be hard-pressed to find a man in the country who wasn't three sheets to the wind after that!"

Annabelle frowned and turned toward the Inspector, who was hiding his eyes under his hand. She turned back toward Daniel.

"So what happened?"

"I prepared everything as usual, and after doing one pig, I heard some loud squealing. Then I remembered that I'd left the pen open. I turned around and saw the other pig streaking away like a thoroughbred!"

"You chased after it?"

"Of course! I damn near ran a marathon trying to catch it, and it still got away when it went into the woods. I've searched and searched for days and nights but I've no idea where it is now."

"I have," Annabelle said, sighing deeply. "I had to swerve to avoid it just a few nights ago. I even saw it on the hills at the back of the church the other morning!"

If ever there was to be an explanation for Philippa's vision, this was undoubtedly one of the strangest, though Philippa would find a drunken butcher chasing a pig a lot less terrifying than a murderous ghost.

"Why is this important?" said the Inspector, stepping forward. "Are you telling me that the reason you're acting so suspiciously is because a bloody pig got the better of you!?"

"My business is my life, Detective," Daniel pleaded, "I could lose my slaughtering license. If this got out, the local gossip would destroy me. I've got competitors who've waited for years for such an opportunity. Meat is a cutthroat business."

Annabelle chuckled. The two men looked at her and frowned deeply, causing her to drop the grin quickly and replace it with a look of embarrassment.

"Reverend," the Inspector said, as he opened the door once again.

Annabelle stepped through it, and they stood closely in the hallway.

The Inspector said, "This has gone nowhere. Daniel's more concerned with stories about an errant pig than a possible murder charge. He's more innocent than I am, and without him as a suspect, we're at a dead end once again. I'm going to close this case and get back to Truro."

"No, wait!" Annabelle said, pressing a hand against his chest to stop him, before removing it with an awkward smile when she realized it was a gesture more intimate than the occasion, and indeed, the Inspector, demanded.

DI Nicholls sighed. "Give it up, Reverend. Sometimes you just have to admit defeat. We've searched the shed, questioned the butcher, and brought in an expert from London to assess the body. There's nothing more we can do. The secrets of that dress died with Lucy."

"Perhaps not, Inspector. Do you have a photo of Lucy?"

Nicholls shot Annabelle a quizzical look, before shrugging his shoulders and leading her to his office, where he sifted through the dozens of folders that had been scattered around his desk.

"I think... Somewhere here...Ah! Here it is," he said, as he handed a photocopy of a picture to the Reverend.

Though the picture was black and white, it was clear to see that Lucy had fair hair, which fell about her shoulders in curls, the epitome of a fairytale princess. She was standing next to a strapping young man, obviously Daniel, her arms around his waist, as he pulled a funny face at the camera.

"How old was she in this picture, Inspector?"

He pursed his lips. "Fifteen years, I should expect. That was taken within a year of her disappearance."

"Hmm," Annabelle muttered.

"Are you quite done, Reverend?"

Annabelle looked up from the photo.

"Not at all, Inspector. And neither are you."

The Inspector frowned his confusion. Annabelle stepped close to him so that he could see the photo.

"How tall is Daniel Green, would you say, Inspector?"

"About six foot on the button, I'd guess."

"And knowing that, how tall would you estimate Lucy to be in this photo?"

"Well, she barely comes to his shoulder. I'd say around five-three, give or take an inch."

"Precisely," Annabelle said, firmly.

The Inspector's confused frown remained.

"The wedding dress?" Annabelle reminded him, though his expression did not change. "There is no way that wedding dress would fit a woman of five foot three, Inspector."

"Are you sure about that?"

"I'm a vicar, Inspector. I've seen more ill-fitting wedding dresses than I'd care to, and I can tell you with certainty that that dress was certainly not meant for Lucy."

"But then..." the Inspector said, trailing off his sentence as he finally realized what Annabelle was insinuating.

"Yes, Inspector. The dress was not Lucy's. It was Louisa's."

"Are you sure?" the Inspector asked, disbelievingly.

"Almost certain, Inspector. I thought it peculiar at the time that Louisa would tend to her sister's wedding dress. Plus the dress itself..."

"Yes?" the Inspector urged, now enraptured by Annabelle's revelation.

"Well, I can't say for sure, but a dress such as that tends not to retain its shape very well unless it's worn occasionally. Especially when it's hanging in a dank cupboard on an allotment. A dress of that elaborate nature would only appear in such pristine condition if it was worn now and again."

The Inspector scratched his chin, shaking his head at the bizarre nature of it all.

"You've lost me, now. I'm beginning to feel like this case will go on forever."

Annabelle sighed, sympathetic to the Inspector's troubled look.

"Either way, it seems like the only thing we can do now is to talk to Louisa. At least to ask why she felt the need to lie to us."

CHAPTER NINE

O NCE DANIEL HAD been released, Annabelle and the Inspector solemnly made their way toward Louisa Montgomery's home. The sun had set, and Upton St. Mary was very definitely experiencing the crisp coolness of emerging autumn.

Whether it was the suspicion that they had perhaps reached a dead end with little to show for it but an embarrassing story of a drunk butcher chasing a pig or the awkwardness they felt over their recent altercation and the revealing of the Inspector's canine troubles, Annabelle and the Inspector drove in silence. DI Nicholls even stayed under the speed limit as he brought them to the brink of what felt like their last chance to understand the truth behind the murder of Lucy Montgomery. Annabelle watched the village that she loved pass by in the passenger-side window of the police car, reflecting upon all the joys, loves, mysteries, and tragedies that occurred beneath its seemingly placid and picturesque surface. She turned back to look at the Inspector and noted the pained expression with which he stared out of the windshield at the road. He didn't seem to notice her. For the first time, Annabelle seemed to recognize the deep concern that had imprinted itself on his face over the past week.

"I'm sure you'll get your dog back, Inspector," she said softly.

The Inspector furrowed his brow for a split-second, before looking at Annabelle and relaxing his face. The worried grimace and cold eyes disappeared like clouds in spring for the first time since he had arrived in Upton St. Mary. He smiled meekly, before turning his attention back to the road.

"Thanks, Reverend. I hope so."

A few minutes later, the detective brought the car to a stop outside Louisa's home. Across the road, Katie Flynn was walking away, having just closed her tea shop for the day. The streets were empty, most people having gone home to squeeze a little more relaxation out of the weekend before the work week began once more.

Annabelle peered at Louisa's house, searching for a light or an open window.

"I do hope she's at home."

"Let's find out," the Inspector replied, exiting the car.

They made their way up the path to her door, exchanging glances all the way. Annabelle rang the doorbell. After a minute of waiting, the Inspector sighed impatiently and rang it again, long and loud. The response, this time, was almost immediate.

"Who is it?" Louisa asked from the other side of the door, her exasperation and irritation evident in even those few, brief words.

"It's Detective Inspector Nicholls and the Reverend Annabelle Dixon. We'd like to speak with you, Miss Montgomery."

"Haven't you two bothered me enough today?" came the increasingly frustrated reply.

"We'd just like to ask you some questions, Louisa," the Inspector said firmly.

"I've said about as much as I'm going to say to you. Now if you don't mind, please leave my property."

The Inspector looked at Annabelle with increasing annoyance.

"We know the dress isn't Lucy's!" called Annabelle suddenly.

The Inspector cast another disapproving look toward Annabelle. He had not wanted them to reveal their hand this early. Seconds later, however, his vexation disappeared, as the door opened ever so slightly to reveal a sliver of Miss Montgomery's face.

"What do you mean?"

Seeing the opportunity, the Inspector decided to take the lead once again.

"The dress that you said was Lucy's; we know that it isn't. And we also know that it's most likely yours."

Though only a little of Louisa's face was visible behind the door frame, her raised eyebrow and concerned expression was clear. She opened the door a little more, cast her eyes around the street outside, and then gestured for the two to hurry in, as if they were the ones who had been dilly-dallying all this time.

They stopped in the hallway as Louisa closed the door and turned to them.

"Well, to the living room! Do you expect me to stand around in my own hallway chatting?"

They duly obliged, settling in to the floral-patterned couch that sat in the middle of a sparsely decorated room. Aside from an old, bulky TV and some elegant glass vases holding dahlias and other seasonal flowers, there was not much to Louisa's house. It was tidy, restrained, full of hard surfaces, and slightly cold, much like Louisa herself, thought Annabelle.

"I hope you do not expect me to provide tea or other comforts for this rudest of intrusions," Louisa said, sitting down carefully on the comfy chair beside the couch. "I would like to make this as short as possible."

"If you would like to make it brief, Miss Montgomery, then I suggest you stop being so—"

Annabelle placed her hand on the Inspector's arm to stop his anger getting the better of him, before addressing Louisa herself.

"Louisa, you told us that the wedding dress in your allotment shed was Lucy's, when that's patently not true. It does seem to be yours. It is your size and appears to have been worn occasionally over the years. Only you could have done that."

"And what of it? I don't see how or why my private property is of concern to your... investigation or whatever you call this harassment campaign you're indulging in."

"It seems rather strange that you would lie."

"Strange?" Louisa said, her voice turning sarcastic and venomous with ease. "Who are you to decide what's 'strange?' Do you make a habit of invading the property of others and passing such impertinent judgments? Personally, I find it rather 'strange' that a leader of the church and a police officer should be conducting themselves in a fashion more befitting the neighborhood gossips. What do you make of that, Reverend?"

"Now look here—" said the Inspector roughly, before Annabelle held him back by placing her hand once again upon his arm.

"It's just that the wedding dress being kept in such a way casts certain doubts upon—"

"In case you have forgotten," interrupted Louisa, "or merely failed to intrude upon that part of my past, I have been married before, Reverend. That is why I have a wedding dress."

The Inspector and Annabelle exchanged one last look. Though he still wore his mask of skepticism, Annabelle could see the defeat in the Inspector's eyes. He leaned in toward her and whispered in Annabelle's ear.

"That's it, Reverend. We don't have anything else on her. We may as well leave now."

"But why would she lie about it being Lucy's in the first place?" Annabelle whispered back.

"The fact remains we have no evidence." The Inspector pulled away, shrugging as he did so.

Annabelle pursed her lips, deep in thought. She had come too far and discovered too much to give up now.

"Is there anything else?" Louisa asked, haughtily, though the question was intoned more like an order.

"There is one thing," Annabelle said, tentatively but with an air of knowing. "You told me you didn't love your husband, Gary. If that was the case, then why would you be so sentimental about your wedding to him? Why would you keep your dress and even wear it occasionally?"

Louisa raised an eyebrow, her face full of stern reproach.

"A wedding is a momentous occasion in anybody's life, regardless of the emotional entanglements therein."

"And yet I see no other signs. I don't see a wedding band still affixed to your finger. Indeed, you don't seem to have any photos of the wedding situated in your house, either."

Louisa's eyes narrowed into tightly wound beams of black light, so intense that Annabelle felt them almost physically piercing her.

"I prefer to keep my sentimentality private, Reverend. What exactly are you suggesting?"

Annabelle galvanized herself against Louisa's formidable and intimidating presence as she prepared to risk everything in pursuit of the truth. She had taken a few gambles already today, and while her instincts regarding the shed had proved fruitful, her assumptions about the Inspector's phone call had been ludicrously wrong. She prayed quickly that what she was about to say would be one of her better judgment calls.

"I believe that dress has never been near a wedding. It was intended to be worn in a wedding that never happened."

"Bah!" Louisa snorted, dismissively. "What utter nonsense! Keep a wedding dress without using it? Why on earth would I do such a thing!? As I said before, Reverend, I was very much married, albeit briefly. That was my wedding dress from my marriage to Gary Barnes."

"Maybe, but there is a very important fact that leads me to believe that that wedding dress wasn't retained in order to remember your marriage to Gary, if indeed it was the same wedding dress you married him in, but for another purpose entirely."

"And what would that be, might I ask?"

"Why would you pack a suitcase of clothes and preserve them just as lovingly as the dress itself, especially for all this time?"

Louisa's eyes narrowed once again, only this time there was a weakness in them, a chink in the armor that Annabelle detected and that spurred her on.

"A suitcase full of clothes," Annabelle continued, her words gathering force as she blustered through them, "makes a strange souvenir from a wedding which has already occurred, but for a wedding that never happened, a wedding for a love that never died, a love that you still, to this day, bear some small hope will be requited, it is oddly appropriate!" She ended with a flourish.

Now it was the Inspector's turn to put a hand on Annabelle's arm. She turned to look at him, expecting him to calm her down, but instead he gave a mild nod for her to continue.

Louisa blurted angrily, "This is ludicrous, Reverend. Almost as ludicrous as the tales you spin in your pulpit. I, however, am not obliged to sit and listen to you 'preach.' I have classes to prepare for, and I believe I have entertained the two of you quite enough tonight. If you don't mind—"

"Answer the question, Miss Montgomery," DI Nicholls said, his voice calm yet strong. "This is not a casual conversation nor idle chit-chat for the benefit of ourselves. This involves a high-profile murder case, one of the most serious cold cases that currently exists in the county of Cornwall."

Louisa said nothing but stared hard at him, her arms folded in defiance.

"Look, Miss Montgomery," the Inspector's voice grew colder, "I've given you the benefit of the doubt. Especially considering that we're talking about your sister, and that you were one of the last people to see her alive. I believed you when you lied to me about whose wedding dress it was, and I've given you a lot of leeway, as you asked, during my questioning. The time has come, however, for you to be upfront with me, with us, now. If you insist on making this difficult, I can quite easily take you to the station and charge you with the obstruction of justice, but I sincerely hope that we can talk about this in a civil, adult manner."

Louisa raised her chin, her jaw clenched so tightly that sharp dimples appeared in her cheeks. She pouted before clearing her throat regally and speaking.

"Very well. If you wish to make this an official matter, I understand I must oblige. Please, then, ask me what it is you wish me to help with, and I shall do my best."

"Thank you," the Inspector said.

Annabelle and the Inspector looked at each other for support in the tense atmosphere of Louisa's living room. They hadn't expected to face such a difficult challenge when they first decided to visit her, but the struggle they were having getting information out of Louisa merely made them feel that there was some truth to be had that was just out of their grasp.

"Did you have feelings for Daniel Green?" the Inspector asked.

Louisa raised her eyebrows and smiled wryly.

"Is this what your investigation is predicated upon, Detective? Teenage hormones?"

"Answer the question, Miss Montgomery."

"I may have had some brief feelings, at some point in time, yes."

"Were you jealous then, of your sister Lucy's relationship with him?"

"Are you implying that I—"

"Stick to the question, please."

Louisa raised her chin once more.

"No. I was not."

"But you were constantly pestering her about the fact that she was seeing him, were you not?" Annabelle added.

"'Pestering'? No. I was her older sister. It was my duty

to ensure that she remained safe and on the right track. Gallivanting about town with cocky boys such as... him... was not suitable for a girl her age."

"So you fought with Lucy a lot?" Annabelle asked.

Louisa's eyes narrowed in on the Reverend, once again spearing her with their sharp beam.

"Sibling disagreements are an unfortunate inevitability, Reverend. I take it you are an only child?"

"Did these fights ever get physical?" asked the Inspector, distracting Louisa from Annabelle.

"Absolutely not."

"Your sister's body showed signs of multiple healed fractures. The pathologist said she'd experienced some pretty bad beatings growing up. You don't know anything about that?"

Louisa paused uncharacteristically before answering this question.

"I..." she shook her head. "No. I don't know anything about that."

The Inspector looked toward Annabelle with another shrug of defeat. They had pretty much gone through everything they had, and Louisa had still retained her tough shell, deflecting everything.

"That's a lot of side-stepping that you're doing, Miss Montgomery," the Inspector sighed.

"Are you implying something, Detective?"

The question hung in the air for a few seconds, fermenting the tension that had reached almost boiling point between the three of them. Suddenly, Annabelle got to her feet, her face flustered and red.

"You know jolly well what we're implying, Louisa!" she shouted, all her good grace and gentleness eroded in the face of the teacher's evasiveness. "You killed your sister!"

Louisa gasped. "This is preposterous!" she exclaimed, her voice full of indignation and surprise.

"Reverend," warned the Inspector.

"No!" cried Annabelle, shrugging the Inspector off as he tried to pull her back to her seat. "This has gone on long enough!" She turned to the seated teacher, who gazed up at her, quietly fuming behind her stony expression. "You fought with Lucy constantly. You were jealous of her popularity, just as she was jealous of your looks. The fights got so bad that they frequently became physical."

"Ridiculous!" Louisa spurted adamantly, but the quiver in her voice was unmistakable.

"But you also became jealous of her relationship with Daniel. You bullied and berated her, hoping that you could force them apart."

Louisa shook her head madly, wincing at the words that Annabelle spoke as if they were weapons tearing her apart.

"You were so madly in love with him, so intent upon a future with him, that you even prepared for the moment that you would have him to yourself. You bought a wedding dress, and packed a suitcase."

"Stop it. Stop..."

"But you just waited and waited. The chance you were looking for never came, and with each day you grew increasingly despairing, tortured not just by your unfulfilled love, but by the fact that your despised sister was the one enjoying the company of Daniel and not you. Until one day, you snapped."

"Enough... Please..."

"What was it? Did she find the wedding dress? Did you simply run out of patience? Did you realize how easy it would be to just—?"

"She knew I loved him!" Louisa screamed suddenly,

interrupting Annabelle so harshly that the Reverend fell back onto her seat upon the couch while the Inspector's jaw dropped almost entirely to the floor.

Louisa trembled in the heavy silence which followed her outburst. She pressed her fingers daintily to the bridge of her nose and pinched it as she struggled to suppress the sobs of her emotions.

"She knew... That's why she was with him... To spite me..." Louisa's sobs grew, her body almost convulsing as she struggled to keep down the twenty-year-old secret, the decades of lies, and repressed feelings.

Annabelle pulled out a packet of tissues from her pocket and handed one to Louisa.

"You will never know...never know what it's like...to bear such a secret...for so long...." Louisa uttered, in between the gasping sobs of her crying. She raised her eyes to meet Annabelle's, but this time the small intense beads of dark light were soft and wet with tears and pain. Her pursed lips trembled maniacally, and the tightly controlled expression on her face softened into the round openness of a broken woman.

"Lucy was popular, but that didn't stop her from detesting me. She always wanted to get the better of me. She'd never had a boyfriend for more than a month before Daniel, but when she realized how much I loved him, she decided to torture me, to keep him for herself, have him hanging around, doting on her every whim. All so that she could rub in my face that the man I loved was hers, and there was nothing I could do about it. Yes. We fought, of course we did. If they'd found my body in the ground, I'm sure they'd discover just as many bruised and broken bones."

Annabelle cast a sorrowful look at the Inspector, but his

eyes were intense and focused, waiting for the crucial moment that Louisa would say what he needed to hear.

"The dress, the wedding bands, the jewelry," Louisa continued, as she swayed from side to side, sobbing and dabbing at her red, wet cheeks, "I gathered them myself in readiness. The suitcase of clothes I packed myself. It's stupid, but I've always been one for preparation. I always thought that if I had a plan, had some money, had every-thing ready, then the final piece would just fall into place. The way I saw it, the way Daniel looked at me, the way he spoke to me back then, I was sure that one day, he would turn up on my doorstep and declare his undying love for me, the kind of love I had for him. In my dreams, Daniel and I would live blissfully and happily ever after."

Annabelle shook her head sorrowfully. "But why, in all this time, did you never simply tell Daniel about your feel-ings toward him? Particularly if they were so strong?"

"I may be passionate, Reverend. I may be proud. But I have always lacked confidence. My mother always told me that I was born out of time. I have never felt it was ladylike for a woman to announce her intentions. It is enough for her merely to entice. Besides," she said, blinking away tears, "rejection would have crushed me overwhelmingly. I daren't risk it. No, he had to come to me."

"What happened, Louisa?" asked Annabelle gently, as she offered another tissue.

Louisa breathed deeply, her face twisted into a look of sadness so deep that Annabelle felt pained just to observe it. With the greatest of struggles, Louisa sat up, tightened her throat, swallowed her sobs, and began talking, her voice taking on a cold, detached monotone.

"We argued, as was typical for us. I told her I didn't want her out too long, she told me she would do as she pleased. It escalated, again, as was usual, and she told me precisely what she intended."

"Which was?"

"To keep Daniel and to stop us from ever getting together."

"That must have made you angry."

Louisa glared at the Inspector through her tears and hurt.

"It wasn't the only thing she said. She called me pathetic for pining after her boyfriend. She ridiculed me. She told me that even were she to leave Daniel, he would never be with a wretch like me for more than a week. And then she left."

The Inspector leaned forward.

"And then?"

"I was so mad. I could barely think. The gall of that girl! To keep us apart simply for her petulant enjoyment! The anger... All the pain... It possessed me. I lost my sense of composure, of rationality. All I could think about was how much I hated her, and how much happiness awaited me if she would only... disappear."

"You followed her?"

Louisa nodded, absently staring at the floor with eyes that were wide and wild.

"I grabbed the first thing I saw – a rolling pin from the kitchen – and then I just ran. Out into the woods. I wasn't even looking for her. I just needed to run. To rid myself of all the anger and passion that flowed through my veins. I ran in the knowledge that there was almost no chance we would bump into each other in those vast woods because, you see, I didn't really want to hurt her. But after a few minutes, I saw her. Walking, so pleased with herself. Smiling, even though nobody was there to see it. She caught sight of me and laughed. She told me once again about how pathetic I was, sprinting through the forest with a stupid rolling pin. She said I was too meek and afraid to do anything. That I was a 'talker' not a 'doer.' Just seeing the smugness in her face, hearing the mockery in her laughter, the ease with which she demeaned me, I lost control. Anger took over once again and...."

Louisa slumped over as she broke down into sobs. This time Annabelle stepped out of her chair and knelt beside the woman, a fresh tissue in her hand. She rubbed her back gently, as more pain was released from the deep well of sorrow that had been residing inside of Louisa Montgomery.

"I hit her. The rolling pin was heavy, and it didn't take much to knock her out, but again and again I hit her until the mockery and the shame was no more. Until the derision in her eyes was gone. Then, I buried her. It was as if I exited my body and watched myself from somewhere above the treetops, clawing and scratching at the dirt until I'd made a hole big enough to bury her inside.

"I didn't do a good job; it was a shallow grave. I lived in perpetual fear that somebody would stumble upon it. Over the years, I would sometimes make my way there in the darkness of the night, to see if she had been discovered. I would talk to her, sometimes. Full of rage, full of regret, full of despair.

"Last month, it was her birthday. I went to 'visit' her, and for the first time I saw that the soil had dried up to the point that her skull was visible. I hurriedly covered it but dropped the apple I had brought. I knew then my secret would be discovered soon. Somebody would find her eventually. I often felt that the fact that nobody had, for all these years, had been the worst punishment of all. To be confined with a secret for so long..."

"'Tell us what happened after you buried her, Louisa," Annabelle gently prompted her as Louisa's words trailed off and she stared out the window, lost in thoughts as deep as the forest in which she had killed her sister.

"I don't even remember anymore. What I can remember feels like something I witnessed, not something I did. I ran back to the house, and when Daniel called to ask where Lucy was, I told him I had no idea. However strange it sounds, I actually believed it. It was the truth. It took me weeks, months even, to realize that what I had done was real and not simply something I had dreamed." Louisa looked up at the Inspector, then at Annabelle. "Has that never happened to you?"

Annabelle looked back at the Inspector, whose face was neutral, but whose eyes seemed wet with compassion.

"Strangely enough, Miss Montgomery, it has. Though the consequences were nowhere near as severe as yours."

Louisa gazed at the Inspector for a few moments, as if finding some respite in her engulfing misery through his words, before the shudders and the sobs overwhelmed her body once again and she began to cry uncontrollably.

"After the original investigation turned up nothing, we all returned to our lives. I got married and went to university. But Gary noticed that something had changed and we divorced," she muttered, in between sobs. "I told people that he had left for America because of his work. In truth, it was because I was unbearable to him. I kept him at a distance even after the marriage. Oh, I was my regular self on the outside, but inside I was dying. I had committed fratricide! I killed my own sister! I was deplorable, deviant. I've hurt almost everybody that was close to me..."

The Inspector stood up and watched Annabelle gently console the teacher as she released years of pain and anguish. He stepped into the hallway and pulled out his radio.

"Raven?" he said quietly into the receiver. "Louisa Montgomery's house... Opposite Flynn's tea shop... We're to arrest her... Yes, turns out she is."

He clicked off the receiver and cast one more look at the despairing woman. Annabelle stood up and joined him.

"Is she going to be alright?" he asked.

Annabelle shrugged pityingly.

"I don't suppose one can ever be alright after committing an act like that."

The Inspector's face settled into a forlorn sadness.

"It's strange. A case like this, a pretty young girl murdered in the woods, it usually gives a sense of satisfaction when you solve it. A clear sense of right and wrong, black and white, good and evil. This though, this is a mess."

They watched Louisa silently for a few minutes. Raven arrived and entered the house eagerly.

"She's in there, Constable," the Inspector ordered, some formality and direction returning to his manner. As Raven stepped past him, however, he put a hand on his shoulder to stop him. "Take it easy. Be gentle with her."

Raven nodded. He carefully led Louisa out of her home into the waiting police car. Annabelle and the Inspector followed. They watched the vehicle make its way back to the police station.

"You seem rather reflective, Inspector," Annabelle said, looking up at his furrowed brow.

"Well, when you hear a story like that, it's difficult not to be. It makes you think about your own life."

Annabelle sighed.

"It's a simple matter of letting go, Inspector. Whether it's a lover, a family member, an idea, or – dare I say it – a dog."

Nicholls looked at Annabelle, his eyes as innocent as a child's.

"And what if there is nothing to replace what you let go?"

"That's just it, Inspector," Annabelle replied, "you'll never know what can replace it if you don't give it a chance."

Inspector Nicholls smiled slightly and nodded his head. He shoved his hands into his pockets and took a step toward the car.

"Would you like me to drop you off home, Reverend?"

"No, thank you." Annabelle looked about her at the nighttime street. "I'd like to pay someone a visit. All this talk has reminded me of a promise I made."

Nicholls nodded, exchanged one more smile with Annabelle, and walked to his car.

EPILOGUE

A UTUMN SWEPT OVER the village of Upton St. Mary in waves of brown. Leaves lay on soil darkened by the increasingly regular rainfall. Where before, the villagers had puttered along the sunny streets slowly, their heads raised in case the opportunity to stop and exchange news presented itself, now they clutched their coats tightly around their bodies and hurried to their destinations.

The faces of the children were no longer red and sweaty from days of physical activity in the hot sun but were sleepy and pale with the return of the new school year and classroom work. The sound of chatter from mothers outside the school gates and raucous banter between men on their way to the pub had been replaced by the sound of wind through dry tree branches and the rustle of crunchy leaves underfoot. Picnics of sandwiches, cake, and fruit had given way to hearty meals of soup, meat, and roasted vegetables. Yes, autumn and the approaching winter prevailed and ordered the lives of the good people of Upton St. Mary as it had for centuries.

"Oh, Reverend," cooed Philippa as she stood beside Annabelle who was leaning over the stove, "I do wish you'd go easier on the pepper."

"A soup with a good kick is just the remedy for this weather."

Philippa shook her head and darted to the other side of the kitchen to cut some bread. She squeezed the loaf, testing it.

"Did you buy this bread today, Reverend? It's lost much of its freshness."

"I did, Philippa," sighed Annabelle, before turning to face her, gesturing with the pepper shaker. "And I dare say that I rather preferred it when you were too frightened by outside "events" to offer me your running commentary on my cooking. I am not a total beginner in the kitchen, you know."

"Oh, don't say that, Reverend. You'll never know how stressful it was. I didn't sleep for a week!"

"Well, if you don't concentrate on your own duties and instead focus on mine, I might just consider hiring Daniel to give you another scare."

"Oh, Reverend, I feel such a fool," Philippa said, as she tossed the bread into a basket and tidied up the crumbs.

Annabelle chuckled as she brought the soup to the table.

"Don't worry, Philippa. You're right, I can't imagine what it must have been like. I don't know what I would have done if I'd seen him at that hour of the night, all bloodied and determined."

"You'd probably have run out and bonked him on the head with a saucepan, Reverend," chuckled Philippa.

Annabelle laughed and mimicked herself bashing someone over the head clumsily when the doorbell rang.

"They're here!" Philippa said.

"Go let them in. I'll set the food out."

Annabelle hurriedly placed the bowls of boiled peas, roasted carrots, potatoes, and parsnips out on the table. Seconds later, Dr. Brownson, Shona Alexander, and her nephew, little Dougie, entered the room, followed by Philippa.

"Hello!" Annabelle smiled, happily.

"Hello, Reverend," Shona said, embracing Annabelle with a warmth that she had rarely seen in the woman.

"How are you?" Robert added, smiling his appreciation politely.

"I'm fine, thank you, Robert. Oh," Annabelle said, noticing young Dougie holding Robert's hand beside him. "And how are you, young man?"

"Hungry!" exclaimed the boy.

Annabelle laughed. "Well you'd better get yourself a place at the table then, hadn't you?"

"We've brought you a present, Reverend," Shona said, exchanging an affectionate look with Dr. Brownson.

"Oh yes?"

Shona lifted the large bag that she was carrying, and with Robert's help, pulled out a canvas. She presented it to Annabelle, who took it slowly and studied it with a big grin on her face. Philippa stepped beside her to get a look.

"It's lovely!" Annabelle gushed.

"It's the church from the hills!" Philippa added, just as stunned by the wonderfully thoughtful gift.

Shona smiled, slightly embarrassed, but pleased with the reception.

"We just wanted to say thank you... for introducing us." Shona turned to smile at Dr. Brownson.

Annabelle looked from Shona to Robert and back again.

"I thought you weren't painting these days, Shona."

"I've started up again," she said, once again looking at Robert, "now that I have someone to paint alongside. But this isn't actually one of mine, Reverend."

"Oh?"

"It's mine," Robert beamed, happily. "Though I did benefit from the advice of an expert," he added, placing an arm around Shona's shoulders.

Annabelle and Philippa looked at the painting, appreciating its detailed strokes and the radiant colors. It showed the church towering magnificently in front of the intricate rows of houses and properties that made up the village, with Cornwall's impressive hills rolling off into the distance.

"Wait a minute," Philippa said, pointing out a spot on the painting. "There are two figures there..."

Annabelle peered closely at the painting. "I believe you're right, Philippa. In fact, isn't that..."

"You and me!" Philippa smiled. "Oh! And even Biscuit is there! Just behind the bench!"

They looked at Robert, who shrugged awkwardly.

"I saw you both there, when I began painting this. At the time I didn't know who you were, but I thought you made a nice addition to the painting."

Annabelle smiled and took one last appreciative look at the canvas.

"Well, you've certainly earned your meal!" Philippa joked.

"I'll just go and put this somewhere safe. Take a seat and help yourselves," Annabelle said as she pottered off, still smiling at the painting. She returned promptly and was about to speak when a shrill sound burst through the restful atmosphere. Everybody turned toward the source – little Dougie. He had his fingers in his mouth.

"Dougie!" Shona exclaimed. "What on earth are you doing?"

Her answer came in the form of the church tabby, Biscuit, as she sprinted into the kitchen from some corner of the cottage, head raised and ears pointed. Dougie whistled twice again in quick succession, at which Biscuit spun around and did a quick circuit of the kitchen table, to the amazement of everybody there.

"Well, I never!" Annabelle uttered in sheer astonishment. "I can barely get that cat up from the couch!"

"I'm training her to be a sheepcat!" Dougie said, beaming with pride. Biscuit sidled up to him, and he promptly stroked her between the ears, causing her to close her eyes with pleasure.

"Wonders never cease," Philippa said, smiling.

"In Upton St. Mary, at least," added Annabelle. "Come on, let's eat. I'm absolutely ravenous."

The diners took their seats, and enticed by the rich smell of soup and the succulent taste of the meat, were soon busily involved in eating away the chill of the weather outside. Young Dougie turned out to have a hearty appetite and ate just as much as the adults, while Shona and Robert exchanged glances and smiles throughout the meal.

"So Robert," Philippa said, as she sat back from the table having just about eaten her fill, "will you be staying in Upton St. Mary?"

Robert finished sipping his wine and placed the glass carefully in front of him.

"I have some things I need to attend to in London, of course." He looked at Shona. "But once that's done, I imagine there's nothing to stop me living here permanently and certainly plenty of reasons compelling me to."

"How wonderful!" Annabelle added, before noticing

the smile on Dougie's face. "And it seems that you've already made a friend here, as well."

Dougie's cheeks went red, but his smile was difficult to hide. He turned to Annabelle.

"Aunt Shona says you have bees."

Annabelle glanced at Shona. "I do, but you won't see many of them at this time of year."

Dougie's face fell, his hopes dashed.

"Still," Robert said, "I imagine we could see where they're kept. You might even learn a thing or two!" He turned to Shona, then Annabelle, "Would that be alright?"

Shona and Annabelle nodded their permission, and Robert stood up with almost as much excitement as Dougie.

"Come on, young fella, let's go. But get your coat on, you don't want to get a cold now," Robert tousled the boy's hair all the way into the hallway.

The three women smiled as they watched them leave, a warm feeling of friendship pervading the room.

"I take it you two have been getting on rather well?"

"Yes," Shona said, somewhat self-consciously. "I must admit, Reverend, when you invited us for tea together, I winced. Blind dates are excruciating."

"I simply wanted to introduce both of you as lovers of painting."

"Oh, come now, Reverend," Philippa said, her smile full of humor. "You knew perfectly well what you were doing!"

They laughed. Philippa placed one of Annabelle's favorite desserts, an apricot tart she had baked, on the table and turned to Shona.

"He's terribly good with children, too, it seems," she added, her smile still full of humor.

Shona looked down at her lap.

"Stop it, Philippa!" laughed Annabelle. "You're embarrassing the poor woman!"

"No, it's fine," Shona said, regaining her composure. "It is actually one of the reasons I've grown so fond of Robert. Speaking of Dougie, it seems that he may be returning to Scotland, soon."

Annabelle gasped for a moment as she absorbed the full meaning of what Shona was saying.

"You mean your sister's getting better?"

Shona nodded slightly, a smile upon her face. "It's not certain – these things never are – but she's certainly making an improvement. She's up and about. If it carries on this way, she'll be well enough to have him back in a month or so."

"Why that's simply wonderful news!" Annabelle exclaimed.

Just then, Robert and Dougie burst into the kitchen again, Dougie having been filled with excitement and energy at the sight of the beehive.

"I saw where they live!" he squealed eagerly, as he ran around the table.

"How did it look?" Shona asked him.

"Scary. Bees are dangerous!"

"They certainly can be, if you don't respect them," Shona replied.

"Do you like scary stories?" Annabelle asked, playfully.

"Gosh, yes!" Dougie replied, his eyes lighting up.

"Would you like to hear one?"

"Yes, please!"

"Come over here, then," Annabelle said, "and I'll tell of a true story that happened to a friend of mine. It's a terrible tale of a mysterious ghost that roams the fields. One night, she woke up and heard a shrieking sound..."

Suddenly, Philippa's face dropped.
"Reverend Annabelle!"

Thank you for reading *Body in the Woods*! Annabelle is a spitfire, isn't she? A lovable one. Her story continues in *Grave in the Garage*.

A corpse in a garage. A puppy in need of a home. Can man's best friend help solve a dastardly crime?

When her beloved Mini Cooper breaks down in the countryside, Reverend Annabelle Dixon is forced to make a stop at Mildred's Garage. But instead of a quick tune-up, she stumbles upon a gruesome surprise... a lifeless hand, peeking out from beneath a parked car.

With one mysterious corpse, two missing mechanics, and a diabolical killer on the loose, Annabelle and Inspector Mike Nicholls may be biting off more than they can chew. Luckily, they have an ace up their sleeve... an adorable little puppy, with a talent for sniffing out clues.

Can Annabelle find the killer before the killer finds her? And can her cute canine friend put the inspector in a better mood? Get your copy of Grave in the Garage from Amazon to find out! Grave in the Garage is FREE in Kindle Unlimited.

To find out about new books, sign up for my newsletter: https://www.alisongolden.com

If you love the Reverend

Annabelle series, you'll want to read the *USA Today* bestselling Inspector Graham series featuring a new and unusual detective with a phenomenal memory and a tragic past. The first in the series, *The Case of the Screaming Beauty* is available for purchase from Amazon and FREE in Kindle Unlimited..

And don't miss the Roxy Reinhardt mysteries. Will Roxy triumph after her life falls apart? She's fired from her job, her boyfriend dumps her, she's out of money. So, on a whim, she goes on the trip of a lifetime to New Orleans, There, she gets mixed up in a Mardi Gras murder. *Things were going to be fine. They were, weren't they?* Get the first in the series, Mardi Gras Madness from Amazon. Also FREE in Kindle Unlimited!

If you're looking for something edgy and dangerous, root for Diana Hunter as she seeks justice after a devastating crime destroys her family. Start following her journey in this non-stop series of suspense and action by purchasing Hunted, the prequel to the series. Hunted is FREE in Kindle Unlimited.

I hugely appreciate your help in spreading the word about *Body in the Woods*, including telling a friend. Reviews help readers find books! Please leave a review on your favorite book site.

Turn the page for an excerpt from the next book in the Reverend Annabelle series, *Grave in the Garage...*

A Reverend Annabelle Dixon Mystery

GRAVE IN THE GARAGE

Alison Golden

Jamie Vougeot

GRAVE IN THE GARAGE
CHAPTER ONE

THE USUAL SENSE of peace and tranquility that beset Annabelle whenever she walked around St. Mary's centuries-old graveyard was not present today. She stepped slowly between the decrepit and leaning stones, her feet heavier than normal as they crunched against the dry leaves and patches of sodden, forlorn grass that even a cow would turn its nose up at. She shivered and pulled her black cassock tighter around her, not yet accustomed to the winter's particularly sharp and sudden chilliness.

Her time as Vicar at St. Mary's Church had been a consistent, daily process of rejuvenation; spiritually, socially, and not least, architecturally. She had taken every care to ensure that the church was a wonderful and pleasing tribute to the Lord, from the luxurious velvet of the kneeling cushions to the inch-perfect preservation of its roof tiles. The shrubbery and fauna that ran all around the church had been carefully maintained and groomed into a flourishing yet orderly arrangement, a delightful array of colored blossoms in summer, and a thick display of sculpted, earthy tones in winter. She had even varnished the mahogany pews and tenderly polished the stained glass windows herself.

The graveyard, however, had remained an untouched thorn in her side. All its residents were a few generations dead, their descendants long-since moved away or neglectful in the upkeep of their deceased relatives crumbling memories. Annabelle had ignored the cemetery during her persistent improvements and renovations to the church, partly because she was loathe to disrupt the time-worn dignity of the area, partly because she had always favored life and vitality over the solemnity of death. But now the graveyard had taken on a wild, unrestrained, and almost ghoulish appearance, she could no longer delay addressing its deterioration.

The gravestones were mostly covered in moss and trailing plants. Some of them so much so that even the names and dates carefully engraved on them once upon a time had become obscured. What must have formerly been a flat, manicured plot of land was now a bumpy mass of mud and weeds. Even the solid, sturdy, iron railings that fenced half the graveyard perimeter were rusted and weather-beaten all out of shape.

The dark, brooding place had long since become a fearful place for children and a source of their horror stories. Now many grieving families preferred to lay the remains of their loved ones in the more attractive and well-maintained plots of a neighboring new town cemetery. There had not been a burial in the church grounds for over a year.

Such a state of affairs was unacceptable to Annabelle. After both a church and town meeting, which nobody seemed to care a fraction as much about as Annabelle, the Reverend put her plan for revitalizing the graveyard to a vote. With a new sense of purpose and the villager's somewhat tepid approval, Annabelle was filled with enthusiasm and optimism as she prepared for yet another refreshing and invigorating project of improvement.

Until she saw the costs.

Fixing a graveyard was a task far too detailed and delicate for mere elbow grease, some hearty volunteers, and a few shovels. Annabelle would need the deftest green thumb to bring its wretched soil back to a state of well-nourished uniformity and the experience of a true craftsman to restore stones in such a bad state.

She pulled a notepad and pencil out from beneath her cassock and intensely studied the figures once more, the wind tossing her hair against her brow as vigorously as her thoughts rushed about her mind.

"If staring at the price made things cheaper," came the warm, lively voice from behind her, "then I'd have a house on the south coast of Spain already. Tea, Vicar?"

Annabelle spun around to see the always comforting sight of her friend and church bookkeeper, Philippa, carefully treading between the stones, a mug of steaming tea in her hand.

"Oh yes, that's just what I need." Annabelle put her notepad away and took the cup.

"You'll catch your death of cold if you keep coming out here, Vicar. Why, you're not even wearing anything warm!"

Annabelle sipped slowly from the mug and gazed out into the cemetery before musing, almost to herself, "We shall need another fundraiser."

"Reverend!" Philippa gasped as she hugged herself tightly against the wind. "We've already had *three* in the past month! The bake sale, the children's talent show, and the raffle. That raffle prize was one of the best I've ever seen,! *A custom-made coat from Mrs. Shoreditch?!* I've never seen such immaculate tailoring. I bought a dozen tickets myself!"

"Then why are we still so short?" Annabelle replied with a tone of exasperation that Philippa knew not to take personally. "We raised more money when we held a flower sale for the path to be re-graveled! I just don't understand it."

Philippa sighed and placed a hand on the tall Vicar's shoulder. Annabelle turned, her face a mixture of confusion and desperation.

"Are people tired of the church, Philippa?" Annabelle asked her friend, as if pleading for an answer. "Have they run out of sympathy for its causes? Maybe it's the grave-yard. Perhaps it's too macabre for most of them to care about. Do they believe the childish tales of ghosts and goblins?"

As the Vicar gazed at her, Philippa opened her mouth as if to say something, before quickly closing it and putting a finger over her lips.

"What?" Annabelle said, picking up on Philippa's hesi-tation. "What is it?"

With an unconvincing sigh of reluctance, Philippa spoke quietly, as if someone nearby might hear.

"Now Vicar, you know I hate nothing more than gossip and rumor-mongering. If I have one sin, it's that I'm harshly judgmental of those who engage in it..."

"Go on," Annabelle urged, stemming the impulse to roll her eyes. Philippa's skills in ferreting out village tittle-tattle were legendary.

Philippa sighed once again. She looked around her care-fully, her gesture adding weight to her words.

"This is probably just idle speculation, of the kind dull

types use to sound more intriguing, and bored types use to fill the time—"

"Come on, Philippa! At this rate, by the time you tell me, I really will catch a cold!"

"Well," Philippa said, unaffected by Annabelle's impatience, "I've heard it muttered in certain circles that a number of families are having financial difficulties."

Annabelle sipped her tea and frowned.

"Doesn't every family have financial difficulties at this time of year? So soon after taking expensive summer holidays, when the heating bills start coming in, and Christmas is just around the corner?"

"Perhaps, Reverend," Philippa said, her tone still conspiratorial and low, "but there's an added element here. You see, a lot of the women are complaining that their husbands are being stingy with money, hiding it. And they're saying the men are spending more and more time away from home."

Annabelle took another sip and frowned once more.

"But is that really anything new, Philippa? The soccer season is in full swing, and it's too cold to do anything but go to the pub in the evening."

This time it was Philippa who frowned, annoyed that her privileged, secretive insights had been dismissed.

"Perhaps, Reverend," she said, in a tightly-controlled tone, "but I just thought you'd like to know what your parishioners were saying."

"I'm sorry, Philippa. You're right. Maybe there is something to it. But financial difficulties or not, the result is the same." Annabelle turned back to face the gravestones. "Without help, this cemetery will remain a sorry state of affairs. If it snows again this year, I daren't think how much worse it could get."

"I'm sorry, Reverend. I'm sure we'll get it fixed," Philippa said, placing her hand once more on the Vicar's arm.

"Thank you for being so positive," Annabelle said, placing a hand over her friend's. "You know, I've taken to coming out here and praying. Even though it's cold and rather ugly, I've always felt like saying my prayers in places that needed them most." Annabelle smiled self-deprecatingly. "I know it's terribly superstitious and silly for a Reverend, but I even find myself looking for a sign. Some sort of signal from the Lord that'll help guide me."

Just then, the air was filled with a low, powerful, rumbling sound. It rolled through the air like a wave before dissipating.

Philippa and Annabelle clutched at each other in shock.

"What was that?!" Philippa squealed.

"I don't know!"

"Did you hear it?"

"Of course I heard it! I wouldn't be grabbing you if I hadn't!"

Once again, the low hum sounded out again, louder and more melodic this time. The two women turned to face each other, their eyes wide and mouths open with awe.

Then Annabelle sighed and chuckled, as more notes were added, and the throbbing sound turned into a moving, atmospheric melody; the distinctive sound of the church organ.

"It's only Jeremy!" Annabelle said, as Philippa let go of her arm and slowly returned to a state of calm.

"So it is," Philippa said, smiling. "He scared me to half to death! It's rather early for him, though, isn't it? He doesn't usually start practicing until ten, and it's only eight."

Annabelle handed her empty cup back to Philippa before straightening her clerical robe.

"I'll see what he's up to. You'd better go feed those pups before they start digging up this graveyard for bones."

"Of course, Vicar," Philippa said, turning away and leading Annabelle out of the graveyard.

"Did Janet give you any word on whether the shelter will be able to house them soon?"

"Not yet, Vicar," Philippa replied, "I shall have a word with her today though, I imagine."

"No rush," Annabelle smiled, "I rather like having them around. Dogs are such happy creatures. I rather think of them as a blessing, turning up out of the blue like that."

"Considering the state of them when they were found, huddled around their mother in the freezing cold, whining like human babies, I rather think they're the ones who feel blessed right now."

They smiled at each other as they went their separate ways; Philippa to the cottage, and its two wet-nosed house guests, and Annabelle to the church and its diligent, early-rising organ master.

"Jeremy!" Annabelle called, over the cascade of notes. "Jeremy! Yoohoo!"

It was only when Annabelle was close enough to Jeremy to wave energetically in his field of vision that he stopped playing, so deeply was he engrossed in his music. He noticed her with a start and pulled his hands away from the keyboard abruptly.

"Oh! Sorry, Vicar. I didn't see you there," he said, in his soft voice.

Jeremy Cunningham was a tall, slim man, his rather pasty face topped with neatly-thatched blond hair. Despite his pale complexion, his blue eyes, and his thin, pink lips that all betrayed his youthfulness, his penchant for thickly-knitted sweaters and sharply-creased trousers indicated a taste that was much older than his twenty-eight years.

"Don't apologize," Annabelle said, "it's rather lovely. If a little macabre at this time of the morning."

"It was Brahm's Requiem. One of my favorites. I tend to play slower pieces in the morning, to warm up my fingers," he said, holding his fingers up and wiggling them with a polite smile.

"Indeed," Annabelle replied, marveling at what she saw in front of her. "I must say, I continue to be amazed by the size of your hands, Jeremy. I've never seen such long and elegant fingers! They are quite extraordinary."

Jeremy nodded gracefully. "My old pastor in Bristol said that 'the Lord provides the very gifts we require in order to worship Him.'"

Annabelle smiled. Jeremy was one of the most devout members of her flock as well as one of the most recent additions. He had moved to Upton St. Mary six months ago and made Annabelle's acquaintance very quickly, presenting himself at the first opportunity in order to offer his services. She quickly found a use for him as the church organist. Jeremy immediately set to work cleaning and repairing the vintage organ. It was a complex contraption, with pipes that reached up one side of the stained glass window on the church's north wall, but Jeremy was up to the job.

Until the dexterous young man arrived in the village, the organ had stood dormant since the death of the previous church organist in 1989. Few of the members of Annabelle's parish even knew the pipes were there until they blasted into life one Sunday morning on Jeremy's command. It caused quite a stir. Postmistress Mrs. Turner nearly fainted, and Mr. Briggs, the local baker, thought he was having another heart attack. They both had to be attended to by paramedic Joe Cox while Annabelle worriedly hovered close by, mentally making note to raise the idea of a defibrillator at the next parish council meeting.

Since then, Jeremy had taken it upon himself to keep the pipes sparkling clean. They often shimmered in the early morning glow that poured forth through the church's colorful windows. Ever the assiduous and attentive care-taker, Jeremy also kept the keys dusted, the pedals oiled, and the wood that encased it all, well-polished.

His accompaniments to the hymns and other musical arrangements were an instant success, adding yet another quality to Annabelle's already popular services. The villagers quickly found themselves drawn to the shy, quiet, young man with nimble fingers who blossomed when conversation turned to the Bible. Some of the more excitable ladies of the village had even taken it upon them-selves to find the bachelor a nice young woman to meet.

For now, though, Jeremy was staying with his grand-mother, a pleasant woman in her nineties who lived alone in the village. Her health had recently taken a turn for the worse, and the support of her neighbors was no longer enough to ensure her wellbeing. Jeremy had left his position as a music teacher in Bristol to care for her during what many felt would be her last stretch on this earth.

"It's rather early even for you, isn't it?" Annabelle inquired.

"I do apologize, Vicar. I would have looked for you, but I saw the door to the church was open and thought it best not to disturb you if I could – though I obviously did!"

"Oh no, not at all!" Annabelle chuckled. "You just startled us. We were standing in the cemetery when you began. Not the sort of place you suddenly want to hear a requiem! I thought the dead were about to rise up!"

Jeremy's face remained solidly blank.

"Nobody but the Lord is capable of such a thing, Vicar, as you well know," he said, in a clipped monotone.

Annabelle's chuckle was quickly replaced with a solemn, serious look. If there had been one deficit in their otherwise easy relationship, it was Jeremy's distinct lack of humor – particularly regarding matters of faith.

"Of course," Annabelle said, in her most sanctimonious of voices. "Well... Carry on."

Jeremy nodded and turned back to the church organ as Annabelle spun on her heel and walked briskly away, her cheeks flushed with red.

Annabelle's discomfiture was quickly dispelled, however, when she stepped out of the church doors and caught sight of Philippa coming from the cottage with two bounding puppies at her heels. Their faces with their large black noses and big brown eyes were framed by pairs of floppy ears that flapped constantly in the bouncy manner of pups. Both tan in color, the female of the two was distinguished by a white streak that ran from the tip of her long snout to the top of her head. The moment they heard Annabelle's feet on the gravel, they quickly ran to greet her.

"*Hello!*" Annabelle cooed cheerily, crouching down to scrub their ears. They yipped and panted their approval. She looked up at Philippa. "Are you taking them to Janet?"

"Yes," Philippa said, taking the opportunity to attach their leashes while Annabelle distracted them with her petting. "For a check-up and a chat. Are you *sure* you want me to give them to the shelter?"

Annabelle pursed her lips regretfully as she continued to stroke the soft fur of the floppy-eared strays.

"Oh, I don't know, Philippa. It's a terribly big responsibility. We would have to buy all sorts of things for them, and what about the flowers? Once they get bigger, they might trample all over the garden!"

"Hmm, they haven't done it yet. They've actually been rather well-behaved for a couple of puppies."

"They certainly have," Annabelle said, giving them one more playful chuck behind the ears before standing up. "But dogs are like people – they have the capacity to do the most unexpected things."

Philippa smiled. "But you do say that it is our duty to help our fellow man when he is in need. I'm sure that applies to dogs too."

"We've already got Biscuit."

"Oh! That cat is never around anyway! Plus she's already taken a shine to the pups. You should have seen them all sleeping together this morning."

"You seem awfully fond of them. Why don't you adopt them?"

"I would, Reverend, but I spend so much time at the church that they might as well live here all the time." She looked down at the two puppies who were standing to attention, their tails wagging, and their big brown eyes fixed upon Annabelle. "Plus they seem to have made their own preference rather clear."

"We'll see," said Annabelle, nodding a farewell and heading to the cottage.

It was still early when Annabelle got into her Mini Cooper and shut the door with the same satisfaction as the day she had first driven it. She settled herself snugly into the seat, drew her seatbelt across her chest, and turned the keys in the ignition. The motor chugged into life, and Annabelle felt a sense of girlish delight emanate from her fingers upon the wheel. As long as she could drive her little Mini wherever she liked, she would be happy; a simple, but endless, pleasure.

The car had always been more than a mere mode of transport for the Reverend. As she spent most of her days either in church or around others, her time in the car was a much appreciated opportunity to enjoy the idyllic landscapes that surrounded Upton St. Mary in solitary contemplation. The fervent beauty of the small, Cornish village and the local countryside had been one of the most compelling reasons to leave her inaugural clerical position in her hometown of London.

The deeply satisfying sensation of being cocooned in the Mini's small yet cozy interior while the exquisite English landscape sped by her window was never greater than during winter. The cold weather made it difficult to take the kind of striding jaunts across endless fields and sun-speckled woods she enjoyed so much in the summertime. However, with the Mini's tiny heater on full blast, and its puppy-esque enthusiasm for the open road, she never felt confined.

In fact, Annabelle spent many happy hours in her car. She had built up a warm affection for the automobile that she lovingly kept pristine. In her more whimsical moods, she could even fancy that it spoke to her. It was almost as though the thrum of its engine indicated its contentment like the purr of a cat, while the gentle squeak of its seat as she sat on it was like a greeting from an old friend. Even the bumps and wheezes of its wheels as it navigated obstacles in the road sounded like the grunts and groans of an old man hurdling an obstacle.

The musical tics and idiosyncrasies of her Mini were like a song she knew intimately, which is why she found herself increasingly bothered by the weak sound of the engine as she made her way to the hamlet at Folly's Bottom. She had intended to discuss the failing attempts to raise funds for the cemetery renovations with a parish council member there, but she had barely reached the halfway point of the five-mile trip when the Mini Cooper's trials grew noticeably worse.

"What on earth is the matter with you?" She pressed the accelerator harder and found the Mini struggling to respond with its typical ready increase in speed.

For the next half-mile, the Mini's engine weakly hummed at an almost inaudible level, occasionally sputtering back into life again with a snap, only to trail off once more. Eventually, Annabelle's fear became a reality – the car stopped entirely.

Annabelle turned the key back and forth a few times in an attempt to get the car started, but the Mini only offered a limp whine in response. Breathing deeply, Annabelle refused to get angry. Instead, she lifted her gaze to the ceiling of the car and silently demanded an explanation from God.

Tightening her coat around her, she stepped out into the chilly wind and closed the door. For a brief moment, she considered checking beneath the hood for the cause of the car's problems but quickly realized that would be of little use. Annabelle's passion for driving did not extend to a mechanical aptitude, and she didn't want to make anything worse. She looked in both directions up and down the road, and with one final huff and frown, she began marching her way back toward Upton St. Mary and the local car workshop and gas station, owned by Mildred Smith and rather unimaginatively named Mildred's Garage.

A short way into her trek, Annabelle decided to take a shortcut and avoid the need to walk along a large curve in the road that went around a farmhouse. She took a small, rough path, fenced on both sides by the fields and surrounding hills. For a few minutes, Annabelle was rather pleased and allowed herself to feel proud of her knowledge of the extensive web of footpaths, lanes, and fields that radiated from, through, and around the vicinity of Upton St. Mary.

Her sense of triumph proved brief, however, when soon into her walk she found the entire way ahead obstructed by a densely packed herd of cows, moving slowly along toward their milking shed.

"Excuse me!" Annabelle politely asked, as she tottered and nudged them to find a gap. "Vicar coming through!"

She quickly realized the animals were – rather rudely, in her opinion – in no mood to let her pass, their stoic faces uninterested in her pleas and their large bodies incapable of moving at a greater speed anyway. Annabelle gazed beyond the large mass of white, brown, and black to find farmer Leo Tremethick at their head.

"Leo! Over here! Leo!" she called, waving her arms frantically like a woman drowning at sea.

The overall-clad figure in the distance briefly turned and removed his flat cap to wave back at the Reverend. Annabelle smiled widely, thinking that the farmer would surely do something to allow her to pass, but instead he merely smiled back, gestured at the cows and shrugged his shoulders apologetically. The meaning was clear – there was nothing he could do. He shouted something which Annabelle couldn't quite make out over the sound of cows mooing and hooves clopping, then turned back to trudge on in front of them.

"I know that you cows are God's creatures," Annabelle exclaimed, as she narrowly avoided yet another cowpat, "But I really must say, you're showing very little respect for the authority of the church!"

For a full twelve minutes, Annabelle inched forward through the muddy, cowpat-filled path behind the herd, pulled along only by the prospect of treating herself to a nice slice of cake at the end of it. When the cows finally turned off into their milking shed, she hurried forward into the junction where the path rejoined the road.

As she made her way to the garage, which was situated on the outskirts of the village alongside one of its largest family pubs, Annabelle found herself with plenty of time to notice her surroundings, including the occasional car that sped by. One of them struck her in particular, a black, sporty Mercedes Benz with dark tinted windows. It was the kind of car one would usually encounter outside a nightclub in a bustling city, so it stood out starkly in this part of the world. The villagers of Upton St. Mary, and indeed, the wealthier families who lived in the mansions and estates surrounding the village, had rather conservative tastes in cars. SUVs, the odd BMW, possibly a classic British sports car, or luxury sedan were the most expensive vehicles that you were likely to find in the roads through and around Upton St. Mary. Most people drove pickup trucks, small hatchbacks, or minivans. The very notion of blacked-out windows seemed preposterous. Annabelle wondered just who could possibly be driving such a car, or even more intriguingly, why they would feel the need to hide themselves away as they did.

Her ruminations were quickly broken, however, when a small van pulled up beside her. She recognized it immediately and walked up to the passenger side window.

"Alfred Roper!" Annabelle called as greeting. "How are you? Off to a job?"

"Aye, Vicar. Busy weekend."

Alfred had become well-known for his wonderful gardening and landscaping skills during the thirty-odd years he had been tending to the grounds of larger houses in the area. He was almost sixty, yet the fresh air and physical nature of his work gave him a fit, powerful bearing. His brown eyes and grizzled beard were rarely accompanied by anything but a pleasant smile, and Annabelle always enjoyed his company.

"But not too busy that I can't give you a lift," he continued with a wink. "Hop in."

Annabelle clapped her hands with glee and eagerly got inside the earthy-smelling van, its comforting warmth making her realize how cold she had been previously.

"Oh, thank you so much, Albert. My car—"

"Broke down on the road to Folly's Bottom? Aye, I just passed it," Albert said in his gruff voice.

"Yes," Annabelle chuckled. "If you could just drop me off—"

"At Mildred's Garage? Of course, Vicar."

Annabelle smiled and settled into the seat.

"Well, I owe you a cup of tea for this at the very least, Alfred. Do drop by the church if you find the time."

"Oh, it's nothing, Vicar, I always offer anyway. In fact, you're the fourth person I've picked up from the roadside this week."

Annabelle turned her head to Alfred with a look of disbelief.

"Really?" she said.

"Aye." He chuckled slightly as he noticed her reaction. "If you ask me, it's all these new *technologies* they keep sticking in the cars. So many dongles and apps and mp3s and i-whatsits – something's bound to go wrong! I don't even trust automatic transmissions, myself," he said, patting his gearstick affectionately.

"But Alfred, my car is a Mini! It might have go-faster stripes, but it's hardly tricked out with all the latest doo-dads, for heaven's sake!"

Alfred shrugged slowly before turning his chin up musing. "Probably the spark plugs then. Yeah. That'll be it."

He pulled the van over to the curb in front of Mildred's Garage and nodded his head politely as Annabelle effusively offered her gratitude and the promise of a cup of tea once more. She waved as he sped off to his next job and walked over to the short, wide building that housed Mildred's workshop.

Mildred's Garage had seen better days. Its paint was peeling, and both of the large metal shutters that fronted the workshop were rusting, but the reputation of the business was spotless. Since inheriting it from her father, Eric, nearly thirty-five years earlier, Mildred had overseen most of the villagers' very first cars, their upgrades to family vehicles, and, for the more successful community members, their luxury vehicles and sports cars. In many respects, Annabelle often thought, Mildred was much like a vicar herself, witnessing and supporting people through the gravest and grandest milestones of their lives.

Though the world had changed and most vehicles were now computers on wheels, Mildred's was still a comforting first port of call for many when a knocking noise started up, a tire ran flat, or a simple oil change was needed. In many respects, much of the garage's popularity was down to its old-fashioned values. People knew they would get a job well done at Mildred's for a fair price – and more often than not, plenty of courtesy and a cup of tea thrown in. She, or her assistants, would even pump gas for customers while they sat in the comfort of their cars, a luxury long since abandoned just about everywhere else in England.

Despite being sixty-two, Mildred was enthusiastic, gnarly, and as strong as an ox – though only half the size. Annabelle marched up the front lot, in between the vintage cars (restoration projects Mildred enjoyed in her spare time), scanning for a glimpse of her frizzy red hair.

"Mildred!" she called, as she drew closer to the garage. "Mildred! It's Annabelle!"

One of the front shutters was open, a small hatchback neatly parked inside. Annabelle noticed the peculiar silence that seemed to permeate the garage. She visited regularly, at least once a week to fuel up, and got regular check-ups throughout the year, but she had never seen it as quiet as this. It often seemed that Mildred spent every waking hour at the garage, hammering or clanking away at some problem or dealing with the phone calls that seemed to interrupt her work every few minutes. On the rare occasions that she was away, one of her assistants would be there: Ted, a grizzled man in his forties who always wore the pained, despondent expression of a man recovering from a hangover, or Aziz, the teenage apprentice who would, to the chagrin of his colleagues, blare hip hop music from a device on his workbench as he tinkered with the cars.

Annabelle stepped into the garage, around the hatchback, and alongside the cluttered workbench.

"Ted! Aziz! Anyone?!"

She knew Mildred well enough to know that neither she nor her assistants would leave the garage unattended. Not without a notice of some kind, unless something was severely amiss. She strode back into the center of the garage, spinning around as she scanned its walls and the two bays.

Apart from the hatchback, there was no other vehicle inside, and with the garage's open plan, there were few nooks and crannies to investigate. Annabelle paced anxiously, keenly studying everything around her for something out of the ordinary.

Just as she was about to go outside and walk around the garage in search of clues, she crouched suddenly and looked beneath the small car in the middle of the workshop floor. It was dark, the lights of the inspection pit beneath the car were off. She strained to remember what such pits looked like. At the far end, toward the back, Annabelle thought she noticed something sticking out. A tool of some kind. She stood up, walked around, and crouched once more to see what it was and whether it could illuminate the mystery of the empty garage.

"Oh dear God!" Annabelle suddenly squealed, pulling back and covering her mouth.

It was no tool.

It was nothing mechanical of any kind.

It was a hand.

To get your copy of Grave in the Garage, visit the link below:
https://www.alisongolden.com/grave-in-the-garage

REVERENTIAL RECIPES

CONTINUE ON TO
CHECK OUT THE
RECIPES FOR
GOODIES
FEATURED IN
THIS BOOK...

ECCLESIASTICAL CHOCOLATE ÉCLAIRS

For the choux pastry:
½ cup water
2 oz. (½ stick) unsalted butter
Pinch of salt
⅓ cup flour
2 eggs, beaten

For the chocolate icing:
2 oz. dark chocolate, broken into pieces
Pat of butter
2 tablespoons water
¾ cup powdered sugar, sifted

For the filling:
½ cup fresh cream whipped with 1 tablespoon of sugar

Preheat the oven to 400°F. To prepare the pastry, put the water, butter and salt in a saucepan and heat gently until the fat has melted. Bring to the boil and, when bubbling vigorously, remove the pan from the heat. Quickly beat in the flour all at once.

Continue beating until the mixture draws away from the sides of the pan and forms a ball: do not overbeat or the mixture will become fatty. Leave to cool slightly. Beat in the eggs gradually until the pastry is smooth and glossy.

Put the mixture into a piping bag fitted with a ½ inch plain nozzle. Pipe onto greased baking sheets, either in finger shapes approximately 3 inches long for éclairs or in rounds approximately 2 inches in diameter for profiteroles. Allow room between each shape for expansion during cooking.

Bake just above the center of the oven for 15 or 20 minutes or until the pastry is well-risen and crisp. Remove from the oven and make a slit along the sides of the éclairs, or in the base of the profiteroles. Leave to cool on a wire rack.

To prepare the chocolate icing, put the chocolate pieces, butter, and one tablespoon of water in a heatproof bowl over a pan of hot water and heat gently until melted. Remove from the heat and gradually beat in the powdered sugar until the icing is thick and smooth. If the icing is too thick, add water a few drops at a time until the required consistency is reached.

Fill the pastry with the sweetened cream, then frost the tops of the éclairs with the chocolate icing. (If making profiteroles, pile onto a serving dish or in individual serving bowls and pour over hot chocolate sauce.)

Makes approximately 8.

DIVINE CHOCOLATE DIPPED
SHORTBREAD

1⅓ cups flour
2 teaspoons baking powder
½ teaspoon salt
¼ cup sugar
5 oz. (1¼ stick) unsalted butter
4 oz. chocolate, broken into pieces

Preheat the oven to 325°F. Sift the flour, baking powder, and salt into a mixing bowl and stir in the sugar. Add the butter, in one piece, and gradually rub into the dry ingredients. Knead until well mixed but do not allow the dough to become sticky.

Roll out the dough evenly on a floured board, then cut into approximately 2-inch rounds with a fluted pastry cutter. Place the shortbread on a lined baking sheet, leaving room between each to allow for spreading during cooking. Prick the shortbread with a fork and chill in the refrigerator for a further 15 minutes.

Bake for 14 minutes or until pale-golden in color. If the shortbread becomes too brown during the cooking time, cover with foil. Remove from the oven, leave to cool slightly, then transfer to a wire rack to cool completely.

Melt the chocolate in a small heatproof bowl over a pan of hot water. Dip the edge of the shortbread into the chocolate and roll your wrist to coat the shortbread with the chocolate in a "half moon" shape. Place on wax paper and chill.

Makes approximately 8.

RAPTUROUS RASPBERRY
CHEESECAKE

8 oz. graham crackers
4 oz. (1 stick) unsalted butter, melted
1 lb cream cheese
2 oz. sugar
2 egg yolks
8 oz. fresh raspberries
¼ pint heavy whipping cream
1 sachet gelatin
4 tablespoons water
Sugar to finish

Put the graham crackers between two sheets of wax paper or in a zippered plastic bag and crush finely with a rolling pin. Put in a mixing bowl. Pour in the melted butter and stir to combine. Using a metal spoon, press into the base of an 8-inch loose-bottomed cake tin. Chill in the refrigerator for 30 minutes or until quite firm.

Meanwhile, make the filling. Put the cream cheese, sugar, egg yolks and three-quarters of the raspberries in a bowl and beat together. Whip the cream until it holds its shape, then fold into the cream cheese mixture. Set aside.

Sprinkle the gelatin over the water in a small heatproof bowl and leave until spongy, then place the bowl in a pan of hot water and stir over low heat until the gelatin has dissolved. Remove the bowl from the pan and leave to cool slightly. Stir into the cheese mixture. Pour into the prepared base and chill in the refrigerator for 4 hours or overnight, until set.

Take the cheesecake carefully out of the tin (the base may be left on if difficult to move) and place on a serving platter. Top with the reserved raspberries, sprinkle with sugar and serve.

Serves 8 to 10.

ANNABELLE'S FAVORITE APRICOT TART

For the French flan pastry:
1 cup flour
Pinch of salt
4oz. (1 stick) unsalted butter
2 egg yolks
2 tablespoons sugar

For the filling:
2 lbs. fresh apricots, halved and stoned
½ cup sugar
1 vanilla pod
or
2 15 oz. cans of apricots in syrup or juice
½ teaspoon vanilla extract

For the glaze:
1 tablespoon arrowroot
1 tablespoon sieved apricot jelly

Preheat the oven to 375°F. Sift the flour and salt into a bowl. Make a well in the center, then put in the butter in pieces, the egg yolks and sugar. With your fingertips, draw the flour into the center and work all the ingredients together until a soft dough is formed. Form into a smooth ball and wrap in aluminum foil or wax paper. Chill in the refrigerator for 30 minutes.

Press the chilled dough into an 8 inch flan ring placed on a baking sheet. Prick the base with a fork. Chill in the refrigerator for a further 15 minutes.

Cover the dough with crumpled parchment paper and three-quarters fill with rice or baking beans. Bake in the oven for 15 minutes, then remove the rice or beans and parchment paper and bake for a further 5 minutes. Take from the oven and remove the flan ring. Leave to cool.

Put fresh apricots in a saucepan. Just cover with water, add the sugar and vanilla pod, if using, and heat very slowly until the sugar dissolves, stirring gently with a wooden spoon. Simmer for 15 to 20 minutes or until the apricots are soft and tender. Leave to cool in the juices, then lift them out with a slotted spoon, reserving the juice. Discard the vanilla pod. If using canned apricot halves, drain well and reserve the juice. Mix with the vanilla essence. Arrange the apricot halves in the flan case.

To prepare the apricot glaze, put the reserved juice (there should be ½ pint so make up to this amount with water if necessary) in a small pan and heat through. Dissolve the arrowroot in a little water, then stir into the juice with the apricot jelly. Bring to the boil and simmer until thick. Cool slightly, then pour over the apricots. Cool completely before serving.

Serves 8.

SAINTLY STRAWBERRY CUPCAKES

For the cupcakes:
1 ½ cups flour
1 teaspoon baking powder
Pinch of salt
4 tablespoons whole milk
1 teaspoon vanilla extract
6 tablespoons of strawberry purée (blend fresh or frozen
strawberries in food processor)
4oz. (1 stick) softened unsalted butter
1 cup sugar
2 eggs

For the frosting:
¼ cup soft butter
3 ½ cups thawed frozen or fresh strawberries
3 ½ cups powdered sugar
½ teaspoon vanilla extract

Preheat the oven to 350°F. Line cupcake tins with paper liners. Sift flour, baking powder, and salt together. Set aside.

In a small bowl, whisk together the milk, vanilla, and strawberry purée. Cream the butter with an electric mixer and add the sugar. Beat until light and fluffy.

Add the eggs and mix slowly until combined. Add half the flour mixture and mix briefly. Scrape down the bowl and add the milk mixture, mixing just until combined. Scrape down the bowl and add the remaining flour mixture. Mix carefully and then divide the batter evenly among the cupcake liners. Bake the cupcakes until a toothpick inserted into the center comes out clean, about 20 to 25 minutes. Cool in the pans for about 5 minutes then transfer to a wire rack to let them cool completely.

To prepare the frosting, purée then simmer strawberries until reduced by half. Beat the butter, sugar, and vanilla extract with an electric mixer. Add the strawberry purée a teaspoon at a time until the frosting is smooth and easy to spread. Pipe each cupcake with frosting and top with a strawberry slice.

Makes approximately 14.

All ingredients are available from your local store or online retailer.

You can find printable versions of these recipes and links to the ingredients used in them at https://www.alisongolden.com/body-in-the-woods-recipes/

To get the first books in each of my series - *Chaos in Cambridge, The Case of the Screaming Beauty, Hunted, and Mardi Gras Madness* - plus updates about new releases, promotions, and other Insider exclusives, please sign up for Alison's mailing list at:

https://www.alisongolden.com/annabelle

BOOKS BY ALISON GOLDEN

FEATURING INSPECTOR DAVID GRAHAM

The Case of the Screaming Beauty

The Case of the Hidden Flame

The Case of the Fallen Hero

The Case of the Broken Doll

The Case of the Missing Letter

The Case of the Pretty Lady

The Case of the Forsaken Child

FEATURING ROXY REINHARDT

Mardi Gras Madness

New Orleans Nightmare

Louisiana Lies

As A. J. Golden

FEATURING DIANA HUNTER

Hunted (Prequel)

Snatched

Stolen

Chopped

Exposed

ABOUT THE AUTHOR

Alison Golden is the *USA Today* bestselling author of the Inspector David Graham mysteries, a traditional British detective series, and two cozy mystery series featuring main characters Reverend Annabelle Dixon and Roxy Reinhardt. As A. J. Golden, she writes the Diana Hunter thriller series.

Alison was raised in Bedfordshire, England. Her aim is to write stories that are designed to entertain, amuse, and calm. Her approach is to combine creative ideas with excellent writing and edit, edit, edit. Alison's mission is simple: To write excellent books that have readers clamoring for more.

Alison is based in the San Francisco Bay Area with her husband and twin sons. She splits her time between London and San Francisco.

For up-to-date promotions and release dates of upcoming books, sign up for the latest news here: https://alisongolden.com/annabelle.

For more information:
www.alisongolden.com
alison@alisongolden.com

facebook.com/alisongolden.books

twitter.com/alisonjgolden

instagram.com/alisonjgolden

THANK YOU

Thank you for taking the time to read *Body in the Woods*. If you enjoyed it, please consider telling your friends or posting a short review. Word of mouth is an author's best friend and very much appreciated.

Thank you,

Made in the USA
Columbia, SC
01 September 2022

66504876R00133